The Voice of the Revolution

"Doc," the voice said, "we need a leader who understands science as good as you do. We've got the organization, but we don't know how to use it."

"Then if I agree to do what you want, you'll get me out of here?" The moment he had spoken, Grayson realized he had said the wrong thing.

"Doc, if you can't get yourself out of here, we don't want you." The heavily jowled face was abruptly gloomy. The thick lips parted and said savagely, "You may recall, Doctor, I told you that if I ever had a bad feeling about you—kaput!"

He raised his voice. "Okay, Hal, kill him!"

Books by A. E. van Vogt

Published by POCKET BOOKS

A. E. van Vogt
RENAISSANCE

PUBLISHED BY POCKET BOOKS NEW YORK

Another *Original* publication of POCKET BOOKS

 POCKET BOOKS, a Simon & Schuster division of
GULF & WESTERN CORPORATION
1230 Avenue of the Americas, New York, N.Y. 10020

ISBN: 0-671-81859-7

First Pocket Books printing May, 1979

10 9 8 7 6 5 4 3 2 1

Trademarks registered in the United States and other countries.

Printed in the U.S.A.

RENAISSANCE

Chapter One

Physicist Grayson heard the peculiar, tiny clicking sound twice in rapid order.

Ping . . . ping—like that.

Very faint.

But what followed was instantly unmistakable. The print he was reading blurred.

Grayson shook his head, impatiently, and drew the contract closer to his glasses. Spots danced all over the page. He sighed, leaned back, and closed his eyes. When he opened them again, he saw the problem.

In each lens of his spectacles, there was a crack horizontally across the transparent "glass," exactly at the pupil level.

He was mildly startled. What an odd coincidence. Both lenses broken within—he now remembered the pings, and realized that that must have been the moment—within a half-second of each other. Being statistically oriented, he considered very briefly the probability of such a simultaneous breakage. The figures that

7

leaped to his mind were so astronomical, and, of course, impossible, that he gave it up.

Silently, now, he removed the derelict spectacles and laid them on the desk. Foggily, next, he searched in one of the drawers, and found a spool of transparent tape—it was, naturally, one of the perfect type manufactured by Haskett Laboratories for specific scientific applications. It had not previously occurred to him to utilize the tape for spectacle repair; and, obviously, he would only use it for that unscheduled purpose until he could obtain a new pair from his eye doctor.

As promised in fine print on the tape holder, the task of repair required instants only. Whereupon, he replaced the tape in the desk, the glasses on his nose— as the door opened and Miss Haskett walked in.

It was her usual vital entrance. She smiled, and said, "Do you have a moment, Dr. Grayson?" With that, her repertoire of pep was gone. She sank onto a chair. And waited with an air of death about her.

Grayson studied the owner of the Haskett Laboratories from behind his glasses. As he did so, an astonishing thought passed through his mind. It occurred to him that he ought to feel guilty about Miss Haskett. Her lonely life cried out wordlessly for love and affection. And who else should answer that call but the man whom she had confirmed as chief scientist when she inherited the business from her late aunt? Theirs was an office relationship, of course. But it had involved just about all of her adult life.

Grayson cleared his throat, suddenly uneasy at the thoughts he was having. In fact, he was so intent on what had happened, he didn't notice the incongruity of what he did next.

He said, "Uh, Miss Haskett."

What he did not realize was the assertiveness of his tone. As if he were the employer, and she the employee. And she was evidently not thinking, either, or was off somewhere mentally. For she said in an absent tone: "Yes, Doctor?"

"What's the name of the eye specialist we use for our male staff?"

"Burr. Dr. Aaron Burr."

Grayson nodded. He remembered it now. His impression that it was an easy name to remember, was correct. He would forget it again, of course.

He realized that his thought had shifted back to Miss Haskett. "What do you do in your spare time?" he asked.

"Oh—various things." She seemed more alert, suddenly.

"Do you read?"

"Sometimes."

"Go to the movies?"

"Occasionally."

Grayson hesitated. The first awareness was coming about what he was doing: asking personal questions of his employer. He had not done that in all their previous association. And he was startled.

Inside him, the withdrawal process was beginning. At which point the woman volunteered, "I live in a condominium complex."

Grayson was startled by the tremendousness of the information. "Alone?" he asked.

A mist of color came into her cheeks. She straightened in her chair. Then: "Alone," she said firmly. And thereafter she did not look at him.

Grayson was silent. He had a feel for tragedy, real or imaginary. He was imagining that she had deliberately roused herself out of thirty-eight years of shyness to tell him that she had the facilities for an affair—a place of her own.

Grayson sighed. He was married, however drably. And he couldn't take the risk of his analysis being wrong. It would be a litle ridiculous if he lost his job or got his face slapped, or—worst of all— was hauled before an Utt commissioner. He was incapable of evaluating all of the consequences of that last.

Thinking of that, shaken by *that,* he said aloud, urgently, "Uh, Miss Haskett, I seemed to have damaged my spectacles. And I'm sure I don't have to tell you that for a male nothing is more important. So if you'll just wait with what you were going to tell me—"

Miss Haskett stood up. "It was about an order," she said. "It can wait." Suddenly brisk, suddenly vital again, she added, "Why don't I just have Miss Broman call Dr. Burr, and make an appointment for you?"

"Uh, thank you," said Peter Grayson, Ph.D., physicist, vice-president of the Haskett Manufacturing Laboratories. He spoke in an absentminded tone of voice, because he was watching Miss Haskett as she went to the door. It occurred to him for the first time in their long business life together that she had a most excellent figure.

As the door closed, he jumped a little. And realized that he had had a forbidden male-type feeling; and that he should be experiencing a strong guilt reaction.

But what he actually felt was a fear of being found out.

Trembling, he sat there in his private office in the scientific administrative section of Haskett Laboratories—

Sat at his special, beautiful oak desk—

And he began to feel better, because he decided that he was not really in danger. The way he reasoned it, the dialogue of Miss Haskett and himself was now gone into that voiceless universe of all the forgotten —because unrecorded—conversations between, and among, human beings.

—She lives alone with her servants, he thought. So she will never mention it.

—And I certainly won't.

His anxiety began to fade.

After all, his momentary lapse was behind him, and was receding further into the past with each instant that went by.

He suspected that what had happened had to do with the cracked lenses of his spectacles.

The possibility was genuinely amazing to Grayson. Could it be that the Utt were right . . . ? On their arrival on earth forty years before, the alien Utt had looked over the human condition, and had diagnosed that the problems of mankind were all traceable to the human male.

From their height of total scientific superiority, they accordingly decreed that every male must take a certain drug at puberty—or later. This drug rendered the individual male nearsighted.

Whereupon, optometrists and other qualified professionals, following Utt specifications, fitted men with spectacles that were ever so slightly rose-tinted. Something else must have been in them, also. Because the lenses of these spectacles, it was said, barred tiny portions of the visible spectrum from stimulating the male optic nerve.

Aside from requiring that all property be owned by women, plus certain transport limitations, and that women were not allowed to take scientific training—an unexplained restriction—that was the only direct Utt interference in human affairs.

What bothered Grayson was that he had secretly dismissed the Utt analysis. He rejected, in short, the Utt concept that men were the villains of earth's tormented history. He had even begun to doubt the history. It all seemed farfetched. And sort of made up.

Suddenly, he wasn't so sure.

He was still thinking about it when Miss Haskett knocked discreetly, and entered. An unfortunate thing occurred. Presumably, she gave him information about his appointment. But Grayson heard only the sound of her voice, and none of the words.

His trouble was, he was intently observing that she was, in fact, a good-looking woman. Totally absorbed, he watched her leave the room. And it was only after she was gone that he thought, startled: When did she say?

He was alarmed now. The situation which he had thought solved had an unsuspected aftereffect. It could —it seemed to—repeat with each visual contact.

He thought: Surely, I'm a litle old for this kind of thing.

Having had that realization, he sat blank for a while. Gradually, a curiosity came—about himself. For a perverse reason, it was years since he had really looked at Peter Grayson. The reason was, he had a mirror in the wall of his office behind him, into which those invited into this inner sanctum could glance surreptitiously while they discussed laboratory business with him.

It had always amused Grayson that buyers of Haskett products could seemingly be hypnotized by their own images in the mirror. Thus confused, they often agreed to contracts that were in his company's favor. (He justified his progressive perfecting of the method by the fact that he, personally, gained nothing from it.)

Satisfied, he clicked on the intercom to Miss Haskett's secretary. "Uh, Miss Broman, will you repeat that information about my appointment with Dr. Burr? It seems to have slipped my mind."

To his considerable satisfaction, the secretary's voice came clearly with the statement that the appointment was for twelve o'clock noon the next day.

Miss Broman, having imparted this welcome bit of information, added quickly, "And Dr. Grayson, one more thing—"

She paused. And Grayson said, "Yes?"

The secretary said, as if to herself, "Oh, here it is." Then: "Miss Haskett asked me to tell you that the address of her condominium apartment is 1818 Mendelian Drive."

Long pause. Finally: "Uh, Miss Broman, see that my appointments for the day are canceled," Grayson croaked. "And tell Miss Haskett I won't be in this afternoon. When I go, I'll be leaving by a rear exit."

He broke the connection. And, after a while, he was pleased to realize that he had kept his wits about him. Because, first, by deciding so promptly to go home, and, second, of course, by going to the side door, he would neatly evade passing Miss Haskett's office in the front of the building.

On the bus—that was one of the transport limitations, men were not allowed to drive; an automobile was considered by the Utt to be a violence-potential instrument—he realized unhappily that his situation was not good at all. In his mind's ear, he kept hearing a feminine sweetness that had been in Miss Broman's voice as she gave him Miss Haskett's address.

One hope remained, he realized. After the lenses were repaired, he presumed that his perceptual ability to hear a female voice with such responsive sensitivity would also rectify.

In short, he would cease to be vulnerable to the unsuspected madness which, he realized, had been lurking inside his skin exactly as the Utt had unerringly observed in human males at the time of their arrival on earth.

Chapter Two

Mila was not in when Grayson walked into the house. Which surprised, him, vaguely. Somehow, he'd always had the impression from her that she never went anywhere during the daytime.

Probably out shopping, he thought. Satisfied with that explanation, he put any considerations of his wife's activity out of his mind.

Straight to his bedroom he went. Placed his spectacles in the drawer of his night table, and lay down. The Utt law required a man to wear his eyeglasses even while he was in bed—but, obviously, to do so with a pair of broken lenses would be tempting further damage.

Surprisingly, he slept. And awakened to the realization that a distant door had opened and shut. Mila, he presumed. There was a silence. He pictured her looking at his hat and cane, where he had left them in the hall, and becoming aware that he was home.

He visualized her instant unpleasant reaction to the realization that he was in the house.

But it was an hour before the door opened, and the rather tall, but slightly stooped woman who had been his wife for over thirty long years came in and stood over him.

"And what is it *now?*" she said in her attacking tone of voice.

It was nearly eight years since his last illness and twenty-two years back to the previous time when he had stayed home after having hurt his hip in a severe fall—and in each instance he had remained in bed exactly one day. Yet he perceived that in her mind the intervening years were as nothing compared to the mental anguish she had endured from his unwanted presence during those two twenty-four-hour periods.

Grayson sighed. For the first time he had the glimmer of the enormous effect the Utt decision about men had had on wives. When man had been named as the earth troublemaker, every married woman became Mrs. Unchallengeable.

Hastily, Grayson told her about his glasses breaking. He was parting his lips to describe how he had temporarily repaired them—when he became aware of a strong chemical odor.

He wrinkled his nose in distaste. "What's that?" he said.

There was no reply. But an amazing thing happened. The shadowy figure, which had towered above him, sank down beside the bed. Though it was difficult to see the details, Grayson had the distinct impression that his wife was on her knees.

And the odor was—if possible—even stronger.

Grayson sat up. "Mila! What's the matter?"

"Don't hurt me!" It was a whisper.

What stopped all immediate overt response by Grayson—his impulse to leap out of bed, his confusion, his feeling that he must instantly go to her aid for something that wasn't clear—was the realization that the odor was a human body smell.

Mila's!

From his early laboratory experiments with animals,

memory wafted a startling explanation. A female animal
in heat had several times affected him unpleasantly.
So much so that, finally, realizing that glandular exuda-
tions were actually too much for his sensitive nose, he
had abandoned his primary interest in biology, and had
gone over to the objective world of physics.

This smell now was like that animal smell then.

. . . A woman in a profound state of sexual stimula-
tion—

He lay back. . . . She sees I'm not wearing the
glasses that keep a man tamed.

Because his brain always worked rapidly, he waited
because he was curious. Then he waited, because if he
told her after such a delay, there was no knowing what
berserk state of mind she would go into.

Vaguely, he recalled the theory of such matters. The
legend was that a few minutes after a man took off his
glasses, their effect wore off. His office experience with
Miss Haskett had certainly proved that.

He was assuming, of course, that the broken lenses
were the equivalent of no-glasses—

After the first few minutes—went on the legend—
a male without glasses progressively became more aggressive, unreasoning, capable of violence.

—To Mila, after an afternoon of no glasses (as she
believes), I must be in some final stage of male insanity.

For her it must be as frightening as meeting suddenly some wild animal: a tiger, a snake, a crocodile,
a shark!

As these rapid thoughts completed, the woman be-
side the bed spoke once more, again in a whisper.
"What do you want me to do? I'll do anything you say.
Just don't hurt me."

"Take a bath," said Grayson, wrinkling his nose
again, "and, of course, you won't be hurt as long as"—
he hesitated momentarily startled by his own temerity,
but the words came anyway—"as long as you do what
I say."

The woman came to her feet with alacrity. "I'll be
right back," she mumbled. Her walk, as she headed for

the hall door, was not steady. But she made it. There was the somewhat prolonged moment when she opened the door itself, and the brightness from beyond flooded through. Then the door closed.

Her bedroom was on the far side of the house from his, a choice of location she had made years ago. Because of the distance, it was always a little difficult to know what faucet she was using—Was she washing her face, or was she under the shower?

Grayson deduced from their dialogue, as the faint water sounds began, that she was taking a bath. He also assumed that she would now have time to recover her good sense. He recalled, uneasily, that a woman who felt herself threatened by a man could ask for instant help.

Yet when the door to his room opened again, he wasn't quite sure what state she was in. She wore her robe; that he was able to detect even with his weak vision. But—what else was not clear.

She came over to the bed, took off her robe, and lay down naked beside him. For long moments the surprise of that was a blankness. Then he felt himself automatically hardening, resisting.

For this woman there was no response in him. Thirty years of abuse tightened the muscles around his heart, and put a cold lump in his lower abdomen—Grayson was mildly surprised at the intensity of his resistance. Normally, he didn't feel that strongly. He recognized that he was aware for the first time of his true feeling.

—I could probably strangle this creature, he thought grimly.

That shocked him. Male violence really does exist, he admitted to himself.

Yet he was fleetingly recalling their sexual past. Several times each year, Mila would go out with certain female companions, and they would all get drunk. Somewhere about two A.M. on such occasions, she would show up in his room, an obscene creature with a tendency to throw up, and demand that he engage in the sex act.

Naturally, and anxiously, he had always come through for her, while she laughed, and belched, and on occasion spat in his face.

In the morning—or, rather, the evening following such a carousel—when he returned from work, she showed no apparent memory of the event.

—But he didn't want her at such times, and he didn't want her now.

"Has Rosie said when dinner will be ready?" Grayson asked, stiffly.

"She said we could eat anytime we wanted to," came the small voice from the bed.

"Oh!" said Grayson. He lay for a long moment, bracing himself. Then he got off the bed, turned on the light, went around to the night-table drawer, got his glasses, put them on, and walked to the door.

There he paused, turned. "Better get dressed," he said gruffly, "and let's eat."

He went out into the hall.

Chapter Three

By the time they sat down at the table, Mila's lean, slightly lined, normally sallow-complexioned face was brick-red. For a while she stared at her plate and did not look at him. And that was somewhat disappointing. He was—he had to admit it—curious.

The truth was, he realized, he was fantastically ignorant and distrustful of Utt judgments, and he craved information on which he could form his own conclusions.

On the surface, what he was doing and thinking looked superficially like men *had* caused all the problems of all time. Because, shortly after the Utt came, women changed.

A married woman, unpursued by her husband, was . . . normally . . . not interested in the sex act. There were reports (from certain salesmen) of exceptions. But the ordinary situation was drably standard. Usually a wife would have a child or two—no more. Since only women were allowed to own property, married women lived confidently. Since Grayson brought home a good

salary from his job, all of which he handed over—
by law—she had a housekeeper—and temporary help
when needed. Her clothes were always neat, her house
clean, she herself always well-groomed. Sane, healthy,
stable, she was the embodiment of a high-standard
human being.

Except for one thing. It was universally observed
that the average wife was as easily angered after the
Utt came as she had been before the Utt. Only now she
really felt free to express that anger.

. . . Good-looking, clean, well-dressed, hard-working,
naturally sexless—but angry— It was the one disturb-
ing factor in a world where men were hard-working,
peaceful, clean, and kept sexually apathetic by a physiologic method that was the law of the planet. For an
unknown reason men in such a condition were never
angry—

Grayson came to that point in his recollection—
when there was a sound at the other end of the table.
His mind jumped out of its reverie. He saw that his
wife was glaring at him. She spoke sharply: "Why were
you not wearing your spectacles in the bedroom?"

Grayson explained about the danger of damaging the
cracked lenses. "But of course," he went on, "I kept
my eyes closed. So I was very careful not to upset the
internal balance."

"Oh!" Some of the high color faded from her cheeks,
and now her lips compressed. It was the old signal
of an imminent flare-up. He spoke hastily, trying to
head off the explosions.

"What you did," he said, "tells us a great deal about
the pre-Utt man-woman relation."

There was a noticeable relaxing of the anger as Mila
said, "How do you mean?"

"Evidently, women offered sex to males out of fear."

"What are you talking about?" The sharpness was
back in her voice.

That startled him. Could it be? Was she trying to
pretend? Was it possible—that she didn't remember?

Forgetfulness. Blankness— Her old pattern. As if it

hadn't happened . . . Of course, he thought, that could be it.

Yet he realized he was still curious and interested, and therefore frustrated.

"Has the fear faded?" he asked.

For a long moment, then, she had the definite expression in her face of someone who intended, yes, to deny. Then: "It was very strange," she said, with a faraway look in her eyes, "what happened. I suppose I should go to see Dr. Austin."

Grayson presumed silently that terror could have a profound physiologic effect. Correlated with shock, no doubt. White blood corpuscles make that jump out of the blood fluid and attach somewhere.

"There I was," his wife continued, "suddenly in a fainting state, and subject to hallucinations. "Can you imagine," she added with a ridiculing laugh, "I actually fantasized myself taking off my clothes, bathing, and then coming into your bedroom without any clothes on." She laughed again, and made an angry gesture with one shoulder. "Probably a regression to my child-bearing state. After all, we've had our two children and our reason for copulation is twenty-five years behind us."

It was Grayson's turn to gaze with a faraway expression. So it *was* going to be forgetfulness.

What an amazing world. In their courtship days, she had pursued him like a sex demon. The vitality she offered him promised that his enforced apathy would be completely overwhelmed by her inexhaustible need. Before marriage, she forced sex as often as three times a day. Afterward—

Two days after the ceremony that, by Utt law, bound them together forever, Mila let him know that marriage was for companionship and for bearing children.

Sitting there, Grayson thought that probably gentler women, like Miss Haskett, lost out in the struggle for marriage because they were incapable of that insane premarital intensity, which absolutely overwhelmed the males subjected to it.

—Too soon to decide anything about that. Yet in a

way he felt a hardening inside him, which was a decision of sorts. That hardening barred Mila from his life.

After dinner Grayson went back to bed, and in his fantasies visualized Miss Haskett in various exotic maneuvers. Far more important, there was a thought in his mind that said there was no danger. Meaning, no chance now of being found out.

About seven, he could stand it no longer. He dressed and went out into the living room. His wife was sitting with her sewing glasses clinging to the bridge of her nose, knitting on another of the interminable sweaters with which she enveloped Mart, who was at college.

"Uh, Mila," said Grayson.

The woman did not look up, did not reply. Which was par, for her. She had ignored him most of their married life, and she was obviously not about to change her attitude now.

"I'm going for a walk," said Grayson. "Perhaps you'd like to come with me."

That was his final hope in defeating the urge that moved him automatically to what was obviously a forbidden adventure.

Something must have penetrated; for Mila looked up. "Whatever for?" Her tone showed surprise. "What's this all about? Where are you going?"

"For a walk," he said.

"Oh!" Then: "No, thank you."

It seemed to satisfy her, for she settled back to the sweater. The last picture he had of her was of her sitting in the chair rocking slowly back and forth.

Outside, Grayson stood peering along the brightly illumined street. The air was fresh, and that braced him. He walked along with gathering confidence. A bus was pulling up at the corner, and because he knew where he wanted to go, he climbed aboard without really considering the future.

He phoned Miss Haskett from the drugstore at the corner of Mendelian Drive. "I happened to be in the neighborhood," he said, "and wondered if you'd care to come out for a cup of coffee."

Her voice sounded breathless. "Why, yes, Mr. Grayson. Why, of course. . . . I—" She broke off. "Why don't you come over to my place?" She said, suddenly calm, "I'll have Joanne put the coffee on. No, I'll put it on. Come to the side entrance."

She gave him directions. And when he got there he had no problem, despite it being a large condominium complex. Trees. Dim lights, and a genuine hidden entrance. An ideal place to visit. From where Grayson stood on the porch of 1818, he could not see the entranceways of the adjoining apartments.

A single touch on the buzzer was answered instantly. The door opened. A vision in white stood in the doorway.

"It's so nice of you to drop by, Mr. Grayson," said the shining young woman.

Grayson blinked at her. It seemed to him she must have made a quick change since his call. Or else he had misjudged this whole situation. "Were you on the way out?" he asked.

"Oh, no, I always dress up for myself at night," said Miss Haskett.

She held the door wider, and Grayson walked in.

They drank the coffee. A silence fell. She sat, empty cup in hand, on the couch. The long skirt of her dress was drawn up primly against the leg nearest him. Grayson placed his own cup and saucer on the little coffee table, and took a deep breath. It was either time for him to go or time for him to do.

His heart was pounding; he could feel a flush in his face. His vision was blurred. He found himself reluctantly agreeing: men really were the villains. For he was clearly in a state of raging desire.

Abruptly, that shamed him. Unsteadily, he came to his feet. "Uh," he said, "uh, Miss Haskett, I want to thank you for this delightful—"

At that point the woman's cup made a clattering sound. She had set it down with such a quick movement that it hit the table, and the cup fell forcefully over on its side in the saucer.

The sound of china on china was startlingly loud in what had been intense silence. Both the man and the woman involuntarily leaned forward to straighten the cup. Thus, bending forward, his head brushed lightly against her hair. It was not physical contact in the real meaning of the word. But in his whole grown-up life, Grayson had only touched one other woman—Mila. And she had made that such a misery—and so rare—that, in fact, he no longer wanted to touch her.

In that peculiar psychic reality of things, it was in actual time several decades since he had been close to a desirable woman. His hand reached for hers, almost knocked the cup over again—but got a hold on her fingers. Then he was tugging her along from behind the coffee table.

It was a long coffee table, alas; by the time he had her approaching its end, his consciousness—conscience —surfaced. He realized what he was doing. He let go.

Grayson stepped back with a sigh. ". . . very delightful," he muttered gloomily, "but I imagine I'd better—"

Miss Haskett had finally rounded her coffee table. As she emerged, she made an uncoordinated grab for his arm, catching his sleeve. And she gasped, "Oh, but you must see the rest of this part of my home."

Slowly, as the tour, with its tiny distances to cover, got under way, Grayson stiffened inside. In many areas he was a supremely analytical person. He saw this journey as a gesture of goodwill by Miss Haskett. They toured the fluffy, very feminine makeup room. The woman explained volubly things about it that Grayson did not hear because he was bracing himself. She took him into a huge bathroom. Apparently, there were special features there; also, that required Miss Haskett to continue her chatter. This time the man had the vagrant thought that this sad little creature had lavished her income upon the furnishings and appliances of a fine home. But, still, he did not hear what those special features were. Something about an unusual method of maintaining the temperature of the bath water exactly at the blood heat of the person taking the bath . . . got through to him.

But that was only one of several items. And that one he promptly forgot as the guided expedition came to a closed door. Grayson never clearly remembered afterward who opened that door. Did he leap forward gallantly and do the amenities? Or was he at that instant still frozen into his single-track thought-feeling-intent?

Whichever—whatever—the door was opened. It was a bedroom. Large. And, again, every expensive. He had a sense of fluffy feminine atmosphere. A king-size —well, at least a queen-size—bed with one of those special headboard and footboard effects: at the head, books, radio, and at the foot (its entire length and height), a built-in, full-size panoramic holographic color television.

They were standing beside the bed, and she was explaining—something. As she talked, Grayson turned and stared at her. He said nothing. He fixed his gaze about an inch above her eyes.

And kept it there.

Suddenly, her own eyes—blue, he observed with a flickering glance downward—shifted. Her voice—which had been virtually unceasing sound—ceased.

"Where's the light switch?" asked Grayson into the sudden silence.

"It can be turned out from the bed," whispered Miss Haskett, "or—over there." She pointed.

"Do you mind?" asked Grayson.

"You're going to turn out the light?" Again she spoke *sotto voce*.

"Yes."

"It's over there," she said once more, and her voice had come up in pitch and had a stricken sound in it.

Chapter Four

A few minutes later—

As, in the darkness, Grayson encountered the nude body of Miss Haskett, he was enthralled. The moments glided by. Skin writhed against skin. Lip pressed to lip. And all was optimum. As the moments lengthened into seconds, and the seconds into minutes, Grayson told himself that Miss Haskett was definitely in a class by herself. Most important, she was accepting him without any apparent reservation. Which, he had to admit, was pretty tolerant of her. After all, she was offering him a nubile, slender, but well-formed, good-looking body. In return, she was having imposed upon her a rather spare, even gaunt, male type with an aging face. The face was fortunately hidden in the three-quarter night of her bedroom. Still, she must know what it looked like, and was making her peace with it.

He decided to tell her how grateful he was for her goodwill. To do so, he removed his lips from hers. His intention was to make the non-kissing period extremely brief; in fact, just long enough to say a few kind words that, he believed, would fit the occasion.

Momentarily, he paused to formulate the words. And, because he was always careful in his uses of English, the moments grew long. And, abruptly, an awful realization that his gratitude had diverted him. And that he was in serious danger of losing his capability of performing the act. Instantly desperate, he fought to save the situation. There was no question about that, either. It was a fight.

"What's the matter?" Miss Haskett whispered.

What could he say? He had virtually wrecked the moment by letting his mind wander to an unfortunate reality: that he was no longer a young man.

As he had that set of despairing realizations, Grayson made a final, desperate effort to salvage the affair, and in a limp fashion . . . succeeded.

It was 11:32 as Grayson climbed aboard the bus that would take him home. At first, as he settled into his seat, the exhilaration and frustration (yes, both) of the evening alternately pulled him up and pushed him down.

But somewhere during the journey came his moment of confrontation:

He had taken an irrevocable step.

He waited for the shock of disaster to move through him.

But what he felt was not that intense. In its place was irritation. He was—he told himself—a grown man, who didn't need any advice from either an Utt or any other living person.

The hostile reaction stayed with him all the rest of the way to his getting-off place.

The emotion had faded a little by the time he entered his house. Yet the prospect of running into Mila did not really shake him. And that was awesome, indeed. Almost a new thought. The idea of a man standing up to a woman's anger with anger of his own was—well—there was no clear reaction that he could produce, having no previous experience to judge by.

But he had seen her on her knees. He had a feeling he would never, no matter what happened, forget the implications of that.

Despite his strong attitude, he moved silently along the dim-lit hallway. In fact, he came to the final stretch, where there was no carpet, he took time to remove his shoes, and then made it the rest of the way in his stockinged feet, turning the dim lights out en route.

After all, he argued with himself, why force problems where none need exist?

In his bedroom, with its door softly shut behind him, he undressed hastily and slipped into bed. As he lay there, then, in darkness, reviewing the night's events, he realized that he was having still another and different kind of thought.

The same scheming part of his mind that had noticed and accepted the little hypnotic ploy with the mirror in his office was busy plotting.

He was remembering what he had once read in one of those awful-example stories, so common in the magazines in the days after the Utt came.

This particular story had depicted a fifty-year-old managerial type very much like himself. In the pre-Utt era—the story had stated—such a man would have had half a dozen mistresses by the half-century mark.

Grayson found himself feeling blank. The story (after his sad performance) seemed untrue. Miss Haskett, all by herself, had been almost too much for him. And, in fact, a definite negative feeling came.

Would he ever again, now that he knew that he might fail, dare take a chance on disgracing himself?

With that . . . moral . . . thought, he must have slept.

Chapter Five

Grayson usually ate breakfast alone; and the following morning was no exception. The maid served him his normal complement of toast, eggs, and coffee. He ate hastily, worried that perhaps Mila might get up and ask him questions.

—Not that I'm afraid, he told himself. Let's just not have problems.

Because of his gulping approach to the meal, he started forth to catch his regular 7:30 bus with time to spare.

The bus stop had its average scattering of sad-looking males already sitting on benches, or standing, each in his own lackadaisical way. Everywhere Grayson looked the reflected light from spectacles glinted back at him. The eyes he saw appeared distended behind the thick lenses. It was very shocking to him this morning, for some reason.

As Grayson walked into this lackluster group, an automobile—which he did not see until it moved—

started forward from the curb fifty feet away. It pulled up opposite Grayson. The rather large, middle-aged woman inside leaned over and said through the open window, in a falsetto voice, "Miss Haskett sent me to pick you up, Dr. Grayson."

With considerable dexterity, and unusual strength for a woman, she continued to lean all the way from the driver's side. Swiftly, she manipulated the passenger-side door from inside, and pushed it open for him.

Grayson was completely taken by surprise. "Miss Haskett—oh!"

He was appalled at his employer's indiscretion. Many of the men who were standing around were neighbors or next-block people. And his hope was that they had not heard what the muffled voice from the inside of the car had said. As he scrambled in, his one thought was to get the machine on its way before another word was spoken.

"Well, that was easy," said the driver. Only now he spoke in a man's baritone. "Welcome to the revolution, Doctor."

The car was moving along rapidly through the traffic, which was light at this hour, consisting essentially—he had read—of unmarried women going to work. And, of course, there was a limited number of working wives.

The first shock of realizing that he was in the presence of a male disguised as a female subsided. And Grayson began the cautious task of gaining the data that would enable him to assess his own situation.

"How long have you been driving a car in this disguise?" he asked curiously.

"Long enough," was the cheerful reply.

"Never stopped for a traffic violation?"

"Well—once." The big "woman" shrugged. "Had to shoot the traffic officer. Too bad, but—" The speaker broke off. "Which reminds me—that will be your first assignment: getting yourself a pistol."

Grayson scarcely heard. His thoughts had already moved forward to the realization that he was asking the wrong questions. And that, in fact, he had somehow been avoiding the crux of the matter.

He said now, boldly, "What is Miss Haskett's role in this?"

The large, pasty face with its artificial cosmetic coloring—to give it a womanly look—grinned. "You were at her place last night, right? We've been keeping an eye on you ever since we cracked your glasses with that high-frequency—well, never mind. Anyway, there you were." Again the grin. "You made it with her, too, didn't you? That's what I meant—welcome to the revolution, Doctor. When a potential recruit goes after a mistress within forty-eight hours—and has the gumption to carry it through to touchdown—that's good enough for us. You're in, and there's no escape."

A pause. Mostly a blankness. A striving to grasp the cruel implications.

It was beginning to be painfully obvious that the other's hearty, almost jovial way of speaking concealed a chilling determination, which Grayson found himself automatically resisting.

He drew a deep breath, for, after all, he had a certain inner power. He was a Ph.D., and a working scientist. He said, "Let's not be too hasty about all these positive statements. If you want my goodwill—which I'm not withholding yet—I suggest you try a little permissiveness, and reason, and an end to threats."

Having spoken, he considered what he had said, and found it good. "That's my statement," he concluded.

The driver shook his middle-aged, womanly head. "Sorry Doc, if you'll think about it, you'll see that we can't operate that way."

"You're *already* talking better," urged Grayson quickly.

The disguised man ignored his interruption: "—We can't operate that way because then we'd have people who would try to suck up to the Utts. So I just have to tell you. If we lose confidence in you, we kill you." He added quickly, "I don't have any feeling yet that we can't trust you. So don't be alarmed. But, Doc"—almost gently—"we don't take chances. When in doubt" —he made a gesture across his neck, then finished— "*kaput*. You see how that has to be, don't you? You're a logical man."

And still Grayson resisted. He was like a man who had accidentally walked into a thieves' hideaway, and as they very reasonably pointed out, they would have to kill him because they couldn't afford to have an outsider know about them. The logic within its frame was perfect. He just didn't wish to be a victim, or—in this instance—be involved.

His reverie ended abruptly as, beside him, the disguised man held out a card, and said, "Anytime you want to get in touch with us, here's how." When Grayson hesitated, the man reached over and shoved the card into his left coat pocket.

Moments after that, the car drew up at the curb. "Well, there's the Haskett factory. Okay, Doctor—out!"

Grayson climbed out, then turned, and said protestingly, "Look!—"

The automobile gave a lurch. The "woman" leaned across the seat, pulled shut the door on Grayson's side, and, as the machine picked up speed, waved—

. . . In the course of the morning, the receptionist put seven calls through to Grayson. "Dr. Pudget on the phone," she would say. Or, "The factory superintendent's on the line." Or, "Can you speak to the buyer for Reid, Leigh, and Ufflegay?—" And, of course, he always could. Because the woman knew very well who he talked to and who could be, or should be, referred elsewhere.

He handled each call by making an initial effort to calm himself, and each time spoke in his usual practical fashion.

He began to feel a lot better.

He was aware of a hardening of his resolve. The truth was, he had been shown a way out from under Utt control. And that way he would now never forget.

So he *was* in the Revolution.

By the time that firmness was in him, it was a quarter after eleven, and time to think of his appointment with Dr. Burr.

Chapter Six

Dr. Burr turned out to be the sturdily built, red-faced man. Over the years, occasional images of such a person had flickered through Grayson's mind, but with no connecting identification.

As usual, because he thought of things like that, it astonished Grayson that one could almost completely forget someone's appearance. Then one day you saw him again. And *that* was who he saw.

Apparently, the entire body and head structure was replayed by the mind; and you could even tell how he had aged and changed. . . . Since a decade had gone by, Burr had moved on to the early forties, with thinning brown hair.

It was this forgotten but familiar person who said, "We'll make the examination first, and then see what happened to your spectacles."

As that stereotyped procedure began, Grayson remembered some thoughts he had had. He asked, "What happens in the brain when a person is nearsighted?"

Dr. Burr hesitated. "Are you referring to the pre-Utt

nearsightedness of a percentage of the population? Or is your question in reference to the Utt chemical method?"

Grayson detected a note in the ophthalmologist's voice that warned him the distinction was meaningful. "What's the difference?"

"The Utt chemical can neither be discussed nor investigated," said Dr. Burr.

"Oh!" Grayson was silent for a moment. Then he said with greater firmness, "No, naturally I'm referring only to the pre-Utt nearsightedness, to which occasionally women are today subject. What is the cause of that?"

The eye specialist shrugged. "Working too hard. Eye demands of modern life."

"Yes, but what happens inside the eye?"

"Unbalanced pull of over-strained muscles. *Fovea centralis* weakened. Complicated."

"You mean," persisted Grayson, "if a . . . uh, woman who was nearsighted rested her eyes every time they tired, she'd have good vision?"

The specialist hesitated. "People are not aware when their vision goes. Don't see an eye doctor till it's too late."

"Suppose this woman rested her eyes for two weeks steady. Would that help her vision?"

"How long has she been wearing glasses?"

Grayson picked a figure out of the air. Since the woman was fictional, he settled on a round number. "Twenty-five years."

"Hmmm, she'd better stick to them, then. The fact is, very little was ever discovered that would lead to a recovery of vision in the case of nearsightedness, and, of course, the subject has not been studied since the coming of the Utt."

"Yes, yes, of course," Grayson agreed hastily. He sat there then, briefly blank. Finally: "I see," he said. "Thank you very much."

He watched idly as Dr. Burr examined the spectacles with the cracked lenses inside a magnification device.

The eye specialist looked up suddenly and said, "You realize this will have to be reported to the Utt."

"Eh?" Grayson was surprised. "I don't understand."

"These lenses," said the eye specialist, gravely, "are made from an unbreakable polymer. There will probably be a hearing on how they got broken."

Grayson heard himself protesting, feebly. "B-but, they just, simply, broke. There was nothing unusual to it."

"I'm sorry," said Dr. Burr. "It's the one thing that's regulated, as you know."

He handed Grayson back the spectacles, saying, "Since you've done an effective repair job, you'd better wear these until your new ones are ready. I'll make it a special, and have them over to you by tomorrow."

He was talking to a man who was trying to visualize having to confront an Utt. Twice, Dr. Burr repeated the instructions. At last, automatically, Grayson took the spectacles and slipped them on.

"But—" he said, vaguely.

Dr. Burr did not look directly at his client. "You will undoubtedly be contacted by an Utt commissioner after I make my report," he said.

"Yes, yes," said Grayson, blankly.

Outside.

Standing, still blank on the sidewalk in front of the building—

Something forgotten poked up into his consciousness. . . . Like an old man—which, he reflected wanly, was pretty close to the way he felt—he reached up with one slightly trembling hand, and drew out of his pocket the card that the man disguised as a woman had slipped into it.

He stared down at a phone number.

Under the number was printed: "Call only in case of emergency."

An infinitesimal dot of returning courage stirred inside Grayson. What brought it to life at all was the realization that in giving him this number, *they* had taken a brave chance on him.

He pictured somebody where that phone was located . . . having to wait there. At any instant, for all that person knew, the police would come.

With so much indomitable will in *them,* the least he could do was let the phone attendant know that something serious had happened.

In the silence of the closed booth, after he dialed, the phone rang twice. Then there was a switching click in the receiver. A pause. Another phone rang once. Then came a second switching click. Once more the phone rang. During the brief silence that followed, Grayson had time to be amazed. And interested.

To his scientifically expert ear, the two sounds spoke volumes. He instantly visualized a relay system. . . . That first click had taken his call and diverted it away from the original phone to an automatic switchboard. The second switching click was to a radio broadcasting relay system.

Even as he had the awareness, a distant receiver lifted. "Hullo!" said a man's familiar voice.

—The man who had been disguised as a woman; his voice.

Grayson hesitated. Small world . . . he was thinking.

What bothered him was that, if Woman-face wore all the hats, then it was also—small revolution.

He suppressed a strong impulse to hang up without identifying himself. Suppressed it because he badly needed advice. And it was a case of balancing his sudden awful doubt against his tremendous need.

—The Utt!

Moments later, voice shaking from the inner conflict, he explained what Dr. Burr had said, about reporting him. The matter-of-fact voice at the other end said, "Thanks for telling us this, Doc. What is Dr. Burr's full name, and his address?"

Grayson gave both.

"Okay," said the voice, cheerfully. "We'll see what we can do. Good-bye." There was a disconnecting click.

Grayson replaced his own receiver, not entirely happy

with the other's carefree half-promise. Still—he had to admit—all problems in the world were not solvable. It was a little difficult to imagine what "they" could do if Dr. Burr had already contacted the Utt Commissioner's office.

Chapter Seven

He went home.

Once again, he was vaguely surprised to hear from the maid that his wife was out. But he was also relieved.

After a while, his mind reverted to his brief discussion with the eye specialist about nearsightedness. It seemed to him that there had been an unspoken truth between Dr. Burr and himself. Since the Utt had a chemical that unerringly created nearsightedness in every male as soon as possible after the onset of puberty, then *they* knew what nearsightedness was.

And, because they could cause it without fail, it was possible they could also un-cause it.

He went to his room, took off his glasses, and looked around him with his foggy eyes. The blur of bookcases, and the wavering desk, and the misty trees beyond the window brought a memory of the way he had been before the Utt. Before he was sixteen. Funny, he hadn't thought of that in, well, in decades.

It had been a bright universe, he recalled, of far horizons, hazed by wondrous blue mists, not by tired, water-gray fog. He swallowed hard, remembering himself as a boy, watching a car snaking up a mountain road to become a tiny dot in remoteness; lying on his back firing with a .22 rifle at a hawk wheeling to the airflow half a mile up, deliberately not aiming at it. Vision he had had that could see the trailing smoke of a jet beyond a distant mountain and estimate its rate of approach.

Grayson put his glasses back on nostalgically. They were, of course, modified by the transparent tape he had used to repair them. But there was still a mild rose-tinted effect.

To have gone through life wearing rose-colored glasses—he sighed . . . and realized he was somehow degraded.

About six o'clock, his wife came in and stood over him. She was fully back in her grim state.

"My eyes ache," said Grayson, who had that story ready.

"Dinner," she said, "is on the table."

The meal was the usual blank.

Outwardly, then, it was a typical Grayson family evening. He presumed that Mila was somewhere watching television and sewing; he stayed in his room, sat at his desk, and stared at a book.

. . . Scared.

The fear had come upon him suddenly when he realized he didn't have the inner conviction necessary for a second visit to Miss Haskett.

After that realization, his deterioration was rapid. He sat there—

Thinking of his forthcoming visit to the Utt—

It was like contemplating insanity. How could such

a thing happen to a perfectly normal, ordinary person who had never in his life harmed anybody?

Later, in bed, he tossed and turned, and slept fitfully, waking up shortly after dawn with aching eyes and a feeling of exhaustion.

Chapter Eight

There was a memo on Grayson's desk when he walked into his office that morning. It said:

> Dr. Aaron Burr's receptionist
> called, and says that your spectacles
> prescription will be turned over,
> with your permission, to Dr. Cyrus
> Flendon, in view of Dr. Burr's fatal
> accident during lunch hour yesterday.
> She says there will, unfortunately,
> be a delay in delivery.

The memo was signed Alison H. And that, and not the message, caught him first.

Grayson stared down at the name, and he felt himself change color. . . . *Alison*. Somehow, Miss Haskett had been alert and had this message channeled through her office. And she was letting him know that he was privileged to call her by her first name.

He was still thinking about when, for the first time, the meaning of the memo itself reached out to him.

Accident? . . . Fatal?

He was instantly thunderstruck. Dr. Burr. Yesterday. Lunch hour . . . why, that must have been within minutes after he—Grayson—had walked out of the ophthalmologist's office.

And after he had called the emergency number—

They killed him.

The repercussions inside him like a ricochet came to a slowing and then to a stop. He sat with narrowed eyes bracing himself to the hard deed that had been done on his behalf.

A thought leaped.

Could it be—was it possible—there was now no record of his visit to Dr. Burr?

He read the memo again, and was swiftly sobered. And saddened. The sadness was not even remotely because a death had occurred. It was the fact that the prescription at least was still in existence. But, of course, that's the way it would be. He had to admit that. Such things were on some active file, and Dr. Burr's secretary would efficiently wind up her employer's professional affairs down to the last diopter of correction, including no doubt checking with the office of the Utt administrator of this area to make sure of Dr. Peter Grayson's appointment with that being.

. . . Or would she?

As he bent over his desk rereading the message once more, Grayson's hope soared. The words about his giving his permission kept shaking him; for they seemed to imply that nothing had yet been done. Hard to believe that . . . and, of course, he would have to have glasses from someone, but—

During the next hour, as he read his mail, he was aware of an occasional excitement. Each time it happened, he pushed it away quickly. But by noon there was a decision in his mind.

At most things he was very efficient, and quite

rational. Normally, he knew what to do about a problem, and did it logically as a matter of course.

There seemed to be no question about what he ought to do about what had happened. All morning his problem was nerving himself to do it.

When he made up his mind, it was because it couldn't hurt. It couldn't make things worse. That was the logic.

Firmly, he called Miss Haskett and said in a voice that trembled only slightly, "I'm going out, and I may not be back this afternoon."

He added impulsively, "But I want to thank you for everything."

There was silence from Miss Haskett, and Grayson took the opportunity to hastily break the connection.

He left by his private exit.

He took the bus to the vicinity of Dr. Burr's office and went up by the elevator. He had only a vague recollection of what the ophthalmologist's receptionist looked like, but he assumed that the woman who was busy behind the desk at the door was the one who had been there the day before.

Grayson had his speech prepared. He gave his name and said, "I was greatly shocked at the unfortunate accident, but I thought I ought to come up and make sure that a certain matter that Dr. Burr and I discussed about my prescription was included in the file which you have suggested should be given to Dr. Flendon."

The woman riffled through her card file. "Oh, here you are." She glanced at it, and Grayson involuntarily slowed his breathing as her gaze darted up and down and sideways over what was written there. Still looking at it, she said, "Perhaps you could tell me what it is you think should be here—"

Grayson held out his hand, and incredibly—it seemed incredible, yet also logical—she gave him the card. He had to struggle against trembling anew as his gaze scanned the document. . . . Right eye—left eye—numbers, figures—astigmatism . . .

But no mention of the damage to his previous lenses,

and no mention of the Utt. Grayson turned the card over. The second side was blank.

"Yes, it's there," he said in a piercing voice. The sound was startlingly loud. Hastily, he handed the card back, and as hastily said, "Is this all? Is there any more besides this?"

"N-no." Her thin face was suddenly puzzled; suddenly the visit must have seemed peculiar to her. But, in the end, she simply shook her head.

Grayson heard his sick voice babbling on. "As you know, these matters are very important to a male; so if you'll have this prescription taken over, tell Dr. Flendon I'd appreciate it if he'd expedite—"

With a terrible effort, he caught the unnecessary words that were still gurgling up inside him, throttling them before they could erupt forth; then he muttered a good-bye and strode out. As he walked along the hallway to the elevator, he grew aware that his clothes were drenched with perspiration.

Chapter Nine

Mila was out when he arrived at the house. Grayson started to nod, started to walk along toward his room—when that information penetrated.

"Out?" he echoed. Involuntarily, he turned. "Where is she?" he asked.

Rosie bridled belligerently. "That's for a woman to know, and a man to mind his own business," she said.

There was a tiny thought in Grayson's mind during the moment after these words were spoken. The thought was a kind of awareness of thirty-plus years of compressed—something . . . finding a way out of a psychic super-heated boiler deep inside him.

He did have one other thought. It had to do with Rosie herself. He had always thought of the housekeeper as being a red-faced, buxom, middle-aged type long past the age of passion, but who—he now reflected —was probably younger than he was.

He made the final evaluation of her from close up. His hands were around her throat, and he was squeezing her neck and shaking her at the same time. As he watched her face turn a richer red and then purple, he bellowed, "When I ask you a question, you answer, understand?"

With that, he gave her a hard shove. They had been in the large hallway, which divided the house into two virtually separated segments—except for the kitchen at the rear. Rosie, thus flung away from him, staggered all the way back to the kitchen wall, and there she sagged to the floor onto her knees. From that position she stared up at the gaunt man who was coming toward her.

During those moments, reason had returned to Grayson. And so it was a concerned employer who walked forward, intending to help the woman to her feet, and to apologize.

Rosie, in her state, was not capable of distinguishing between the berserk who had attacked her, and the appalled man whose only thought was to help her.

She started to cry, a wailing sound. As she sobbed, and wept, and begged for mercy, she also said things about Mila, and where Mila was, and what she was doing, that Grayson didn't clearly hear. Nor, for the moment, was he interested.

It took him a good twelve minutes to calm his emotionally shattered employee. Several other minutes were taken up, as he led her to her bedroom, and onto her bed. After he had gone out, and softly closed her door behind him, Grayson heard a sudden sound. A key turning, a lock clicking. Rosie had locked herself into her bedroom.

That brought a small resurgence from the psychic boiler. But the feeling was more a sense of the unfairness of things. Not one bit of remorse for what she had said. Not, apparently, a single awareness that what she had got was long overdue for a thousand similar minor insults.

Suddenly, he was wishing he had asked her to repeat where she had said Mila was. But—with a frustrated swallow—a little late for that. . . . He stood there, striving to recall the bits and pieces of Rosie's sobbings and moanings on that subject. But it was impossible. Something about Mila being a guide, and going out at one o'clock every day.

He had a feeling, from the tone of the enforced admissions, that whatever Mila was doing, and wherever she was, was specifically a woman thing.

For want of knowing what else he should do, Grayson retired to his bedroom.

He had a feeling that there would be consequences to his outburst, and so he lay there mentally vague, and slept twice, and did not awaken the second time until Mila came in to tell him that dinner was on the table.

All through the meal, his wife's face held a pallor that he had seen briefly two nights before, but never previously in their long life together. It was a dark discoloration; splotchy, not even.

Gradually, Grayson came out of the gloom that his act of violence had plummeted him into. He grew interested in the spectacle on the other side of the table.

Toward the end of the meal, Mila said without looking at him, "You don't believe those wild things that Rosie said about me."

Since Grayson didn't remember what those "wild things" were, he held his peace.

His wife continued in a voice that trembled, "The poor woman was so terrified she repeated a plot from a recent movie she saw."

"What movie?" asked Grayson.

"How would I know?" A tiny bit of color had come into Mila's face, and her voice had in it a touch of her long-practiced rage. She added, with asperity, "The things people say when they're being tortured they don't always remember afterward."

Grayson was silent. He cautioned himself against making any admissions. He realized that, in a perverse way, he was enjoying the game. It occurred to him that he was really in quite a strong position. . . . *She thinks I know what Rosie confessed.*

It was an amazing situation. He had never been in such a one-up condition in their entire married life. He wondered, in a kind of haze, what she could possibly be involved in that was so important for her to conceal from him.

What made the game possible was that he didn't care. Not a used razor blade. Not a piece of torn, sticky tape. Not a single discarded container. It didn't matter.

It struck him that it was time that he did make a remark. "What puzzles me," he said, "is why you took Rosie into your confidence."

The woman flashed, "You've got to talk to somebody. You can't spend your whole life in silence . . . never saying anything to an intelligent person."

The outburst penetrated the man. The penetration was instantly so deep that he had time only for a passing awareness that what she had said was an admission that she *had* taken Rosie into her confidence. The failure to reject his accusation established that there was something to confide and, therefore, confess.

Grayson muffed the opportunity. The thirty-plus years of her withdrawnness was a bigger event than any current madness.

"You could have talked to *me*," he said.

"*You!*"

The word was explosively emitted. Her lips were parted, as if other words were about to fire forth. But at that instant she must have had some cautionary thought of her own.

She swallowed, and when she spoke it was in noticeably a different tone, a controlled thought. She said, "Anyway, the whole thing is ridiculous, and I don't want to hear another word about it."

Grayson said, "You brought the subject up."

"I could see what you were thinking," she said, instantly impatient with his simple truth.

Grayson was completely in control of himself, though sadly realizing that he was not going to learn her secret. Too bad. The thought he had was that all these wives were reflecting the Utt-guided world, fulfilling their own twisted lives in some way that no male had ever thought to investigate. He hadn't. And he had heard no rumors, either.

A question remained in his mind. How did one close off a conversation like this? He considered what he did know, and that was what he referred to.

"I haven't decided yet what I'm going to do about this," he said. "In future, tell me when you plan to go out daytimes, and where."

The rest of the meal was eaten in silence, with a pale-cheeked woman at one end of the table, and a baffled man at the other.

Since he hadn't learned details, it was scarcely a victory.

The rest of the evening was typical Grayson family separate existence. Each of its two principals retreated to their side of the house. And Rosie stayed in her behind-the-kitchen retreat.

Grayson toyed vaguely with the idea of visiting Miss Haskett. But there was another thought, a puzzled-at-himself thought: Really, this is ridiculous. I am not that kind of a person. I have a wife who was just as lost as I was in all this Utt nonsense. Maybe now we can straighten things out. . . . He retired at his regular hour of eleven o'clock.

About ten minutes after Grayson turned out his light, the door to his bedroom opened. There was a light in the hallway beyond, and silhouetted against its brightness he saw that the person who had opened the door was Mila.

She had on her robe, and in the brief glimpse he had of her, she looked very much as she had two nights before. . . . She came in quickly, and closed the door.

In the consequent darkness, he could hear her bare feet padding across the floor toward him.

Pause.

Abruptly, there was a shadow beside the bed, and a tugging at the blanket. And the feel of cool air as the sheets were lifted.

Moments later, there she was in the bed, under the sheets, only inches away. Silence settled—Was she lying there in the nude? Had she been drinking? Was he now expected to go through the hideous experience of making love to a drunken woman?

He could hear her breathing in the near night.

"Peter." It was a small voice, tentative. "Are you awake?"

Grayson hesitated. Then: "Yes."

"I'm lonely, Peter."

Grayson did not move. He felt remote from those words—and from her appeal. It was too long. She had been too much of a bitch, one of millions of wives who had done all those incredible automatic things against men. . . . He was a male, psychically castrated by the Utts. Along with other women, she had proved for all time that one woman, or a billion, was, were, totally incapable of responding to a man so defeated. Not once in all those years had a single, understanding thought penetrated into that feminine brain.

And, obviously, at this moment she was reacting at some sub-level to the change in him that must now be apparent.

Grayson was appalled as he considered the implications. Pre-Utt human history said that men had used their greater physical strength without mercy to subjugate and control women. And it was to such threat of control that women responded.

And nowhere a sign of human intelligence doing anything more than acting as a vague guideline in a generalized legal fashion. Down where the sexes confronted each other, life operated at an abysmally primeval strata.

"Peter, I don't want to be over there on the far side of the house anymore. I think it's wrong—"

A critical note in her voice. As she spoke, those words struck Grayson. *Just a minute,* he thought, *just one minute. Is she implying somehow that I put her over there?* He felt an instant outrage rising up in him.

Yet, after a long moment, he suppressed the feeling, because—well—because it was only *another* automatic behavior.

It would be a little difficult, he argued to himself, where behavior was one hundred percent automatic, to disapprove one automatic aspect of it more than any other automatic.

He was still thinking about it when there was a movement of the bed and of the quilt. The next moment her nude body was on top of him; and he was being subjected to a sincere embrace.

It was very convincing. Kisses as in the days of their courtship, except her mouth felt a little different. Perhaps an age difference. And her body seemed less firm. But even as he had the awareness, he also had a repeat of the thought that maybe having a personal intimacy with one's wife was, in fact, the best solution.

It took awhile. Negative thoughts kept intruding. There was one long period when he simply lay still and waited. And had the gloomy thought that his future activity had, indeed, better be restricted to Mila because other women would surely not tolerate a male who kept collapsing into semi-impotence.

Yet, though it took time, he presently completed the act. Whereupon, exhausted, impervious to what may have happened to Mila during all these minutes, he rolled over and went to sleep.

Grayson awakened in pitch darkness with a thought. . . . Only one problem remained: What would he do with the Revolution. . . ? As he lay there, the inevitable logical reality of that configuration also moved through his mind. Consciously, he braced himself. It seemed to him that his purpose with The Revolution had to be limited.

Save himself from it. Nothing more.

Extricate, evade, hold away—

He assumed it was impossible to defeat the Utt, who had conquered a mightily armed earth, almost without a shot being fired.

Therefore, concentrate exclusively on defeating The Revolution, and that only in relation to himself. Which, surely, he, who knew so much, and they so little, could do.

Chapter Ten

His new spectacles were on his desk when he got to the office. There was also a memo from Miss Haskett: "I have passed Dr. Flendon's bill on to the accounting department with instructions to send him a check. Underneath was the signature, Alison H.; and there was a P.S., which asked simply, "Is this good-bye?"

Grayson stared palely down at the final three words. But finally he picked up the spectacle case, removed the glasses, and stared at them.

A choice.

Put them on, and have all those intense feelings fade into the passionless world that seemed unbelievable now when he looked back. But, still, the memory of those apathetic years was there in his mind. They *had* happened.

The alternative: not put them on.

Actually, of course, it was not a problem. This was a decision he had made in the wee hours of the previous night.

With abrupt renewal of determination, he replaced

the new spectacles in their case, and slipped the case into his inside breast pocket. Then he sat examining the cracked lenses so skillfully repaired with the tape manufactured by his own company.

The crack was not easy to see in either lens. Relieved, he headed for his own workroom.

He spent most of the morning in that private laboratory putting together an apparatus. Shortly after noon, he was ready. Firmly, he got himself an open line on his switchboard and dialed the number that the man who had dressed as a woman had given him.

Once again he listened to the click of the switching machines, as his call was relayed through a radio sender. As before, a voice came on; and what was thrilling about it, and what stopped him for the time of several heartbeats, was it was not the same voice.

The man repeated his query: "Yes?" More sharply.

Hesitation ended. Grayson pressed the button that activated the special mechanism that he had constructed.

It was a long-ago, forbidden method. Somewhere in the Utt takeover, it had got lost in the minds of a few scientists. It had a brief flourishment in the power struggles between and among certain giant corporations and, of course, countries.

The method had originally interested Grayson, sufficiently for him to follow it up, exactly as the mirror did later, and for the same reason. Naturally, this approach, since it was mechanical, did what it did, invariably.

It transmitted a high-frequency sound complex along the wire through the ears of the listener into his brain. It stirred the hallucinatory mechanism. Told it stories, which it evoked from the subject's own memories. Moved him thereafter in a fantasy that was as real as . . . real.

Grayson watched a needle on his specially constructed apparatus. It moved—suddenly. Immediately, he closed a relay.

And had his permanent, directional location neatly locked in.

Grayson took off his work clothes, and dressed, whistling under his breath. Large thoughts bounded around inside his head; and in the vicinity of his jaw was the energetic sensation which, for want of a better term, he had always labeled his "chin-up" condition.

At such moments, he modestly acknowledged that the physicist—himself—who had contributed numerous inventions to the Haskett Manufacturing Laboratories was, in fact, a minor genius. Out there were a lot of people who didn't understand the laws of Nature as he did. It would be ridiculous if he permitted them to control him.

He had to admit The Revolution's determination and its ruthlessness still exceeded his by a geometric multiple. But maybe he could fight even if he didn't commit murder while doing so. Much as one played a game of chess, he could fend them off while he sharpened his tools for whatever developed.

It wouldn't be the first time, according to historical accounts, that a small power had by a fierce show of capability convinced a belligerent neighbor to leave it out of its aggressive calculations.

—All I want is to go about my own business. . . . Surely, it was a small goal, not unachievable.

He took a bus, of course. En route, in his "chin-up" condition, he thought about that critically for the first time. Shook his head abruptly. No, no. That would be veering. It would be going along with The Revolution against the Utt. Such, he reminded himself, was not his purpose.

So, no car for him.

Oliver Street, he discovered ran north and south, pointing toward some low hills at the south end. It was an old street, he observed, as he walked along it. As far as his gaze reached, the street consisted of old, two-story residences. Every house looked lived in. On such a street, neighbors must know each other, and must therefore be wondering about the occupants of number 477, his destination.

—Well, that was their problem. . . . Grayson went briskly up the veranda and rang the doorbell. The man who presently answered was a slender fellow about five-feet-nine, age about thirty-five, with dark, haunted eyes and a bushy mustache. Obviously, *he* didn't ride around passing himself off as a woman.

The almost black eyes brightened as Grayson spoke the key word. The man's slim hands reached out, and pulled Grayson inside. "My dear brother," he said huskily. He embraced the physicist, murmured several times, "Mike, for God's sake, where have you been all these years?" But his hallucinatory programming required no reply.

Grayson was anxious. "You're still here by yourself?"

"Yes, yes, it's my shift. As I told you, next shift is due at six P.M. We can talk—" He broke off. "Oh, oh, there's the phone. Just look around, Mike." He departed hastily along the hallway and through a door that opened and closed. After a few moments, Grayson heard his voice as a distant, murmuring sound.

What bothered the physicist was that he did not believe a subordinate knew all of the precautions that the killers of The Revolution had taken. So the sooner he accomplished his purpose, the better.

Despite his sensational success, he was, he realized, still keenly disappointed. What an unfortunate outcome for his first attack; capturing the mind of a stranger instead of the man who had been his initial contact with The Revolution.

Chin up. Later for him.

He stood in the hallway; and to his right was an open doorway into what must have once been a living room. Grayson glanced through it, and was startled to observe that it was a small auditorium that looked exactly like the inside of—yes—a church. The rows of seats were, in fact, old pews. On the walls were enlarged photographs of people—all women, he realized—in a kneeling position. And there was a rostrum at the far end of the room, with a small electric organ on one side, and a minuscule stage on the other.

A door beyond the stage caught Grayson's roving gaze. He walked through to it. It opened into what had formerly been, and possibly still was, a library. There were books on shelves that ran the length of one side, and there was a large desk, and two settees, and floor lamps.

Grayson headed for the desk. It looked to him like headquarters. The drawers, as might be expected, were locked. But he inserted a thin, needle-shaped, powerful magnet, and twisted its considerable pull around until the simple mechanism that locked each drawer in turn clicked open.

He took it for granted that he had no time to examine contents. Therefore, he merely glanced at and through and around, and picked up a motley assortment of papers and instruments, and shoved them into his pocket.

Next, he pulled out one of the drawers completely. Into the empty space he placed his combination microphone and destruct system. The instrument was so tiny that he was able to push it a few inches with the end of a ruler, which he found in the drawer. Then he lost it.

It didn't matter. He shoved the drawer over it, and stepped back. His feeling: main purpose achieved. Strong impulse to leave. Take no chances.

But stubbornly he shook his head, and thought: No. I should look this place over. Including going upstairs. But—first—another door leading to a side room.

Grayson entered cautiously. He believed in his method; but he also kept reminding himself that the slender man might not have been alone at the moment of attack.

The room he found himself in was large and nicely furnished. Grayson realized he was surprised by its elegance. Somehow, he had pictured the "revolution" as being on the poverty side.

He had stopped just inside the door; and now he sent

quick, seeking glances to all the corners. Desertedness confirmed. Hurriedly, he walked forward, glanced behind settees, around tables, and through another open doorway.

That door led to a room with machinery in it, and—as he stepped into it—he saw also the metal paneling and other objects that had the look of being electronic equipment. His brother sat in a chair at an equivalent of a telephone switchboard. His back was to Grayson, and he showed no awareness that anyone had come in.

The physicist withdrew as silently as possible, and thought: Full circle . . . He had come all the way around the ground floor. Presumably, he could have gone on through, past the man on duty, and out through the hall.

He preferred to go back the longer, roundabout way. And so up the hall stairway.

The upstairs: bedrooms. Pretty ordinary. The first three were ill-kept. More like what he had expected the whole place to be like. Whoever slept here, on arising carelessly pulled the over-quilt into some kind of symmetry, adjusted the pillows slightly, and departed. In one room, slippers and socks lay on the floor. In another, a pair of pajamas had been hastily stuffed into a drawer, which had been left partly open. In a third, the closet door was open; inside was a jam-pack of disarranged clothes. Only the fourth and final bedroom, the one in the rear, was neat and clean and well-kept.

Presumably, this old house was the headquarters of The Revolution. The leaders slept in these bedrooms. Three-quarters of those leaders were proved by their living space to be inelegant types.

Outside at last. Softly Grayson closed the door behind him. And so along a near cross street to where a bus came presently.

And he was away. Safe.

He hadn't really thought about the effect on himself of a successful foray. But that there was one he grew aware of as he sat in the half-empty vehicle.

A trembling deep inside. Excitement. And joy . . . For heaven's sake, Grayson argued with those feelings,

I had to do this—it was as if somebody had threatened to hit him (which, in essence, they had). And so he had a right to hit back. In self-defense.

What a nightmare if he had actually let them bully him into doing what they wanted. Then the risks that they would require of him would be enormously greater than what he had just required of himself.

Chapter Eleven

Back at the plant he continued to breathe deeper than was normal for him. There was, he realized, a heavy thought in his mind: It isn't over. This isn't over. . . . One more thing, at least, he had to do.

The problem was simple enough. Who had cracked his glasses? From where? Somewhere in the building near him. Which meant a member of The Revolution was an employee of Haskett Laboratories.

Let us surmise, decided Grayson grimly, that it was someone who had been recently hired.

It occurred to him that today was not a good day to go to Miss Haskett's front office and, in the course of a conversation, ask that he be supplied with a list of personnel recently hired. Today, still, he didn't want to confront Miss Haskett.

—Why not make my own investigation first? Then I can ask more intelligent questions.

Shortly before five he phoned home and told Rosie to tell his wife not to expect him for dinner. At five there was the usual noisy rush of departing staff. The whole place emptying in a span of ten minutes. During those minutes Grayson stepped for precaution's sake into his private bathroom. That was in case Miss Haskett remained behind and looked in on him with some excuse.

In fact, while he was inside the locked bathroom, he did hear the door of his office open, and presently shut. When he emerged at five-thirty he seemed to be in an empty building. Doggedly, Grayson made sure of that. Walked along corridors, glanced in to all the work-rooms, as well as the main office *and* Miss Haskett's large office overlooking the street.

Progressive relief then. Every location was indeed un-occupied. With, of course, one exception: the caretaker, Fred Gross, was in his cubbyhole at the rear of the building.

Grayson returned to his own office, sat at his desk, and with his eyes measured the distances and directions from which the energy that had cracked his lenses had to have come.

Whatever it was had been aimed. It hit his lenses exactly. Aimed from where? Sitting there, Grayson strove to recall how he had been holding himself.

He was also remembering that one lens had broken a perceptible instant after the other. So somebody had focused a machine from just about—right there.

There, Grayson was bemused to notice, was a wall behind which—he knew—was a storeroom with a lock on its door. It was on a corridor that ran parallel to the front of the building. And it just so happened that sel-dom had he personally had any reason to use that particular hallway. Pretty smart, pretty observant, for a new employee. The main passageway to the factory was connected to the general offices by a corridor that extended at right angles to the locked storeroom.

Grayson was at that door by the time he had the de-tails reasoned out. He tried various keys from his key-ring on the padlock, had became progressively irritated as none fitted. A grim feeling. Who had put in a lock and failed to send up a duplicate key to his office? That would have to be explained.

Despite his ire, he also had a slight feeling of ironic amusement. All the locks in the Haskett Laboratories were a complex kind, not vulnerable to magnets or other tools of thieves; he who knew so much had seen to that.

Frustrated, he returned up front and phoned Fred Gross. That brisk individual, a mustached fifty-year-old type, ambled in a few minutes later, examined his own key ring, and shook his head. "Better ask the owner," he said. "She authorized that lock to be put in last week at somebody's request."

"You don't recall whose request?" asked Grayson, calming down considerably.

"No—sorry. One of the technical people, I'm sure."

That was for sure, all right. Nobody else but a "technical" expert, and certainly not Miss Haskett, would have the knowledge needed to crack the Utt-designed glasses.

"Okay, Fred," said Grayson, "we'll get the details tomorrow. See you later." He finished casually with a lie: "It's not important."

After the door had closed behind the other, and Grayson was alone again, he continued to stand there in that swank office of his with its huge mirror so cunningly arranged and its delightful paneled walls; and what amazed him was his own image in the bright, silvery glass. His lips were drawn back. His teeth showed in a half-snarl.

Startled, he walked closer to the mirror. It did not seem to be quite the same face as he had gazed at that first day. The color was higher, redder. The gray eyes glittered. And his mouth—savage, animal-like.

First thought: Feeling like this, can I wait? He decided, no. A second, less happy thought: I suppose this will require another infidelity with its impotence and incapability. But he picked up the phone and dialed Miss Haskett's number. When the soft voice came on, Grayson explained that he had come back to the office to finish off some work.

"Was wondering," he concluded, "if I could drop by your place for a cup of coffee on my way home."

When he arrived, she was in a filmy dressing gown, all frills and blues and pinks. She said, "I had just taken a bath when you called. It seemed silly to get dressed for a cup of coffee. I hope you don't mind."

Her words had the sound of a good beginning for a man who expected to pay a price for what he wanted. Yet, as they drank coffee, Miss Haskett suddenly became aloof. "Where were you the last two nights?" she asked in a strangely tense voice.

Grayson was mildly surprised at the accusation in her voice. Then: "Home," he said, "of course."

His simple reply did not have the effect he would normally have anticipated. Miss Haskett continued to gaze into the wall off to his left. There was a rich, pink color in her face that matched a portion of her robe. "With your wife?" she asked in a strained tone.

Grayson hesitated, baffled. He had been at home at night with his wife for nearly thirty years, which—he did a mental calculation—came to roughly eleven thousand nights. It was difficult for him to grasp that suddenly an additional night or two was considered significant.

But his mind was already grappling with the intent he divined in her words; and so he was able to say, "She in her part of the house, and I in mine—why do you ask?"

He was gazing at her face as he spoke. Her features remained clean and straight. All the elements for attractiveness were visibly still there. Yet her normal good looks were marred now by tension.

And then, as he continued to watch, the rigidity . . . dissolved. Swiftly, her expression changed from accusation through a kind of laxness to grief. Tears spilled out of her eyes and rolled down her cheeks.

Simultaneously, her lean body under all that flimsy clothing twisted toward him. In the next split-minute she had somehow managed to slide partly over into his lap, and her face was against his chest, and she was murmuring something that sounded like, "Oh, darling, I love you, I love you."

It was a surprised and resigned Grayson who partly carried but mostly led an unresisting Miss Haskett into the bedroom, and into the bed. And there, after duly removing all the clothes of both persons present, he tried to treat her as the word "mistress" implied. As he had anxiously anticipated, it was not easy. But he found that by thinking about his reason for coping, he was able to brace himself, and, more important, was eventually able to complete the transaction.

Afterward, he said casually, "I know I could ask you this tomorrow, but I might forget or be too busy. A certain key—"

After he had explained there was silence in the darkness beside him. Finally: "I'm thinking," said Miss Haskett.

Her next movement occurred when she pulled away from him; and he heard her climb out of the bed. He was aware of her making movements in the pitch night of the room. Abruptly, the light went on, and there she was dressed in her robe again. She poised beside the light switch at the door.

"You get dressed," she said, "while I look through one of my keyrings. I'm beginning to remember about this." She left the room with a gliding motion, closing the door behind her.

When Grayson emerged a few minutes later, she held a key out to him, and said in a contrite voice, "I'll have to check in the morning who the man was who put the lock on. I think it was one of the new people."

Grayson was ready to depart. So he accepted the key, glanced at it, noticed in his perceptive fashion that it was, in fact, a key for the type of padlock on the door, and said, "When was this?"

"Oh, just a few days ago. He came and asked for one of our locks. I gave it to him. He installed it himself, and brought me the key. Naturally, I know that because of your work you should have access to the whole building, and I should have had my secretary make you a duplicate. But all this happened between us—I'm sorry."

Grayson acknowledged the explanation with a kiss.

A few minutes later, he stood at a lonely bus stop, watching the lights of the approaching machine; and he thought: —I suppose I could wait until morning to check on this matter.

He was actually sitting in the bus, gazing absently out at the passing night scene, when the weakness of that decision penetrated. Instantly, there was no doubt about what he should do. . . . Until I'm free of The Revolution, there must be no delays— They were infinitely determined. So must he be.

He got off at the next stop, and in less than half an hour was walking along the partially lighted approach to the long, wide, one-story brick building with the great glass windows, above which towered an illuminated sign displaying the name: HASKETT MANUFACTURING LABORATORIES.

Chapter Twelve

He could see dim lights through the glass of the door as he let himself into the building. First, he phoned Fred Gross, since the opening of the front door at this hour would trigger an alarm. A minute later he unlocked the door leading from the office section to the rear, found himself in darkness, and was fumbling for the light switch—when someone grabbed him.

Total surprise!

Fear. Shock. And a kind of horror. He was conscious of being half-carried, half-dragged through a doorway. Startled realization came. It was the door that led into the previously locked storeroom.

As he had that awareness, the extreme anxiety in Grayson took a shape, a direction. He had the distinct conviction that his being taken into such a place was dangerous for him. The certainty came that he would be murdered and locked in there.

He had been grabbed from behind. Now, belatedly, he sought to brace one foot against the floor. With the other, he kicked to his rear with every bit of strength that he had. His heel struck a shin.

It must have been precisely as severe a blow as Grayson had intended. Inches from Grayson's ear, a man's hoarse voice cried out in pain. His grip, almost steel-hard up to that moment, relaxed.

Instants after that, Grayson had spun around and grabbed his erstwhile captor by the shoulders. The man grabbed back, groped with one hand for Grayson's neck.

The struggle there in the darkness was shocking. The attacking fingers had him by the throat now, and were squeezing remorselessly. Grayson ceased his futile pushing, and with every ounce of strength grasped the wrists behind those fingers. At that moment twenty-three years of daily push-ups paid off, for he was able to maintain his strength.

His fingers tightened, and pushed, and pulled, and twisted. Not easy. He had the unpleasant impression of a sturdy body, taller, larger, heavier than his. Yet suddenly his own ability to endure and persist brought an ending. His assailant abruptly gave him a shove. And retreated.

Grayson, who had no plan, let him go. In fact, his initial feeling was relief. He heard the other's rapid footsteps, and then the office door closing. The physicist had a mental picture of the man running across the main office section, and so out of the front door of the building.

Undecided, still willing for the man to depart, Grayson fumbled through the still-open door of the storeroom, and this time located the light switch. The flood of illumination that lighted the hallway made it possible for him to re-enter the outer office quickly. And so he had a fleeting last glimpse of the back of a well-built man in a dark suit. There was a momentary impression of a mass of blond hair.

Instants after that, the retreating figure made it to the street, turned left, and disappeared. Grayson made sure the outside door was locked. Then he went back into the rear and so into the storeroom. He located the light switch, and presently was staring at some twisted, burned metal that lay on the concrete floor. A fierce heat still radiated from what, on cautious inspection, proved to be a fused mass.

By measuring its position, he was quickly able to deduce that this was probably the machine that had cracked the lenses of his glasses; and, sadly, somebody had got to it minutes ahead of him.

Now what?

He sagged into a chair, and realized: —I'm tired. I should be in bed. . . . But there was another reality in him. Not a new idea, but powerful for all that.

—It's not over. Somebody out there is still thinking about me. Therefore, I shall have to think about them.

He was startled to realize, despite his exhaustion, that he was having an extreme esoteric thought: It was time someone who knew something took responsibility for the state of the world.

What was startling was that the person who, at this moment of irritation, he had in mind for the role was— himself. For the mere seconds, then, that the image of Physicist Grayson as *the* savior of earth was in his head, he felt an inner change. A brightening. An expanding. An upness.

Human power, he thought, wryly.

As swiftly as it had come, the feeling yielded to a more prosaic, intermediate purpose. Wearily, he realized what he could do to protect himself from these various people who were trying to force him into their thing. Reluctantly, but with a sense of having no recourse, he headed for his personal laboratory.

There were two solutions to his problem. One required the simple but time-consuming task of sewing a dozen or so small chemical—both liquid and gas— containers into the lining of his suit, each complete with its flexible tubing and method of spraying it directionally from either a sleeve or a lapel or a button.

The second method was even more complex. Inserts. Those tiny devices, which, when attached to a blood vessel or a nerve end, either acted as additional senses or injected a chemical into the body to counteract any of several types of standard attack techniques.

Putting them in, and making all those fine adjustments, would require a good portion of the night even for a knowledgeable person like himself. But it had to be done.

His wife was in his bed asleep, when Grayson, having undressed in the hall, stepped gingerly into his bedroom, and so into the bed beside her. Because of the dozen or so plastic inserts in various parts of his body and head, he slept awkwardly. He kept rolling over onto one or another of the intruding items, each time awakening from the unaccustomed pressure.

In the morning, at breakfast, he instructed Mila to go out and buy a gun—"for the household" was the way he blandly put it.

"Where were you last night?" she asked in a plaintive voice. "I waited up for you until midnight."

Her attitude—the way she sat, the expression on her lean face—was not assertive; she was not being difficult. It was an emotional complaint, and did not require a verbal answer. Grayson answered it by getting to his feet, walking around the table, and kissing her on the lips. Minutes later, as he was leaving, he called back from the door, "We'll take care of each other tonight."

He left the house with the distinct male feeling that his home situation had become normal. His decision was that he would try to keep it that way. No more Miss Hasketts.

It seemed to him that . . . "All I've still got to deal with are these damned people who are trying to involve me in their madness."

Thinking about it, as he sat peacefully in the bus, he was impressed by the feeling that it was not an unsolvable problem.

Chapter Thirteen

The Utt Commissioner requests your presence on a 7-B matter.

Time: 10 AM Friday,
January 22, 2023 AD
Place: Utt Building, Utt Square.

Report to Basement Information.

The official-looking document continued to lie on Grayson's desk after he had read it. An indeterminate number of moments later, he had the surprising thought—for him—that, okay, it's going to happen.

It had been a good try. But, evidently, Dr. Burr *had* phoned the office of the Utt Commissioner for the area *before* going out to lunch.

Grayson glanced at his watch: 8:24 AM, Friday the 22nd. They didn't leave you much time. Suppose he hadn't come to work today.

He stood up. The action was partly automatic and partly a reflection of another thought. Better phone The Revolution. The impulse to do exactly that brought wry amusement. All his evasive action was now proved useless. Well—he made a conscious qualification—almost useless. Never, he told himself, discount a win. It could be that at some later time his ability to visit the headquarters of The Revolution would be valuable.

With that reassurance, he returned to his desk, picked up the phone receiver—and then paused again. Should he also use the call as a means of controlling whoever answered *this time*? A rejecting feeling came. Asking for help required a certain purity of motive. Later, when this was over, he could resume his escape program without having to be conscience-stricken.

In a way—he had to admit it—such fine points were irrational. But how else did anyone maintain any degree of personal integrity? His decision continued to seem right, as he dialed the secret number. There was the usual pause, then the single ring, and then the first distant switching sound. And then—a woman's voice said, "I'm sorry, you have reached a disconnected number. Will you please check your phone book, and try again?"

Grayson broke the connection with a jerking movement. Somewhere inside him, the icy calm that he had somehow been able to maintain all these minutes cracked. A tremor went through the lower part of his body. For many seconds, then, he fought a silent battle with an impulse to dissolve into a thing that shook and shivered. There was even a small period of time when he heard a low moaning sound.

Startled, Grayson whipped around to see where it came from. And realized the disgraceful truth: Good God, that was *me* making that noise!

The shock of the recognition ended the worst part of his reaction. He gulped several times. And to a degree, then, was himself again. But he was critical. His feeling was of having betrayed the stronger, braver Grayson who had surfaced for the first time a few days before.

All right, here he was in this predicament. He! Not anyone else. In a little over an hour, *he* would be standing, or sitting, in front of an Utt. *For the first time in his life,* he would see an Utt face to face.

Absently, as he had that awareness, he reread the citation, and this time the code term made an impact on him: 7-B.

"A 7-B matter—"

As a long-time reader of official documents, contracts, and printed forms, Grayson turned this one over expectantly. The code list was there. He scanned it with the speed of an expert, and came swiftly to the explanation: "7-B—a basic violation. Be prepared for a thorough investigation."

Sitting in the bus ten minutes later, Grayson tried to turn his attention away from the inner world, where the fear of a thorough investigation resided like a large, unpleasant lump. As best he could, he concentrated his attention on glancing in little jumps and jerks of eyes and head to the watch, then away from it and out to the street, and then back again. Each time, the feeling grew stronger that the street was not moving by fast enough in relation to the time.

Grayson climbed off the bus seven minutes before ten, and walked swiftly to Utt Square a block away. He had of course been there before—when he was much younger. That time, a quick walk through the square, a rapid scan of the Utt building, and then off down a side street, relieved somehow that he had made it. As if there had ever been any doubt.

There were stories that said you could run into an Utt on Utt Square. In fact, Grayson had heard that wives of missing Utt-hating males sometimes waited here and tried to waylay Utts, demanding that their husbands be released, or at least that they be given information as to their fate.

Utts, confronted by frantic wives, defended themselves by rising up into the air and floating there on some—it was said—magnetic principle. The requests of the wives were never answered. The males inquired after were never seen again.

Grayson, himself, had not seen an Utt on his one

previous visit; and he saw none now, as he hurried toward the entrance of the Utt building.

The buliding itself was a single-story structure with a rather ornate, windowless front. A plastic sign rose up from the roof. It had on it the words: OFFICE OF THE UTT COMMISSIONER. The entrance was a large, heavy-looking door.

The lack of windows and the solid opaqueness of everything that was visible had had a chilling effect on Grayson during his original speedy—so to speak—flyby.

Now, the solidity stopped him. Literally, he came to a halt. Stared with slightly glazed eyes at the closed door, and the hard, blank walls of the building itself.

A memory came. Himself as a small boy, at school. The teacher threatening him for talking. *Stay in at recess,* she had said grimly, *and I'll settle with you. . . .* His seat was at the rear of the room, near the exit. As she faced the blackboard again, like a silent thing of the night he had slipped from his seat and out the door and was gone—home to mother.

Standing there on the street at the entrance to the Utt building, with people sounds all around—a bus hissed past; a car steamed up to a nearby curb; several women climbed out of it, chattering—Grayson thought: This stopping was as automatic as his long-ago reaction to that teacher. Only, this time there was no mother to go home to, and to accompany him to school the next day.

He was on his own in a world which would now—what? He had, he realized, no idea. What would the procedure be? Suppose I don't report to the Utt Commissioner? Suppose I just go back to my laboratory (an equivalent of returning home to mother) and resume my activities—what will happen? Who will come for me?

Rather startling to realize that he knew of no clear-cut method that could be used against him. There *were* women police who controlled traffic. This had proved necessary because a percentage of women drivers had a tendency to ignore mere traffic signals at the rush hour.

Traffic control was not of Utt creation. The women's associations, which ran the city and county governments, had inaugurated the procedure, and the Utt either didn't notice, or made that much compromise with their theory that men were responsible for all the problems on earth.

Would a traffic policewoman come and try to arrest him—if he didn't show? Grayson felt suitably blank, as he contemplated the possibility that, maybe, only fear in men kept the entire Utt control going.

Even as all those thought-feelings poured through his mind, he observed that he had automatically taken hold of the entrance latch. And that, despite the possibilities he was fantasying, he was not seriously considering rebelling—as he worded it to himself—"at this time."

With that, he consciously tugged open the door.

Chapter Fourteen

Inside was brightness. A high marble foyer, of the kind common to government buildings—where space was often wasted. From the foyer, a wide corridor led to barely visible elevators. The elevators were hard to see because a woman sat at an information desk directly across from where Grayson had entered, and she and her stand blocked the view.

It looked quite normal. Grayson was (somehow) relieved.

With that feeling, he let go of the door through which he had come. But he looked back and watched it close. After it had clicked shut, he reached tentatively toward the latch. He stopped the movement, because . . . Do I really want to know if it's locked? He decided, no.

There was, he realized, a philosophical implication to his negative decision: If you're in prison, better not know it. Human beings had been unconsciously living by that creed since time immemorial; so it seemed to

Physicist Grayson, as he started forward across the floor.

The woman at the desk was middle-aged and matter-of-fact. She read his "summons," handed it back to him, and pressed a button.

Pause. Complete silence. And then a man came out of a door beyond the elevators. He came quickly toward Grayson. "This way," he said.

He was a small, stocky individual with wavy brown hair and tame brown eyes behind his glasses, and also middle-aged. Grayson followed him into one of the elevators, watched as the man pressed a button marked with the figure 1, but said nothing, as the door glided shut, making only the faintest sound as it did so.

During the seconds these actions required, Grayson's mind had been trying to analyze the meaning of the number, 1, on the control button. It couldn't mean one up, since he had quickly observed that the high ceiling inside completely filled the space which, outside, he had estimated to be the exterior height of the Utt building. So, therefore, it must be going to a basement office. Which fitted: *Report to basement information!*

The apparent reality of that provided him with about a minute of optimism. In that minute, the elevator descended several hundred feet. And it kept on going down.

The realization that there were vast distances below ground level was such a new thought for Grayson that he was fascinated. These Utt had really burrowed into the planet. No wonder no one ever saw them. Presumably, they were living in buried cities.

In many ways, it was a pleasant and unthreatening journey. Soft music played from hidden speakers; kind of lulling. Grayson listened to it. Then he glanced at his guide, or guard (whichever), and he said, "Will I be coming up this way?"

The brown eyes regarded him somberly. The wide shoes shifted on the corrugated floor. The chunky body made a gesture as if a thought had moved through the mind behind the stolid face. Verbally, then, the man did not reply. But he shook his head slowly back and forth in the time-honored meaning of no.

During that interchange, another minute had gone by. The passage of so much time—and distance—evoked from Grayson a reluctant realization: Really, I have a basic decision to make.

Since that moment in his office when first one, then the second, lens of his eyeglasses had cracked, he had been fighting a delaying action. It had been like having a purpose not of his own choosing. In effect, it had seemed—he must make his way out of the predicament created for him by the broken spectacles. No feeling in those early stages of deciding anything.

True, he had grabbed at Miss Haskett, and accepted a sort of reconciliation with Mila. Those were decisions. But they weren't like making up your mind to do something basic. Obviously, if this was not his way back, it would have to be by way of another elevator shaft like this one. Which really meant, if *they* didn't bring him up, he would have to do it for himself.

And *that* would be absolutely basic.

As he had the awareness, there was a faint sound from the vehicle in which they had been dropping so precipitously. At once it began to slow. Yet at least another minute passed before the elevator finally stopped.

Grayson drew a shaky breath, as he mentally reviewed the journey, and came up with an estimate of how far the machine had brought him: *half a mile!*

He was still contemplating the fantastic implications of such a distance when the door glided open. Beside Grayson, the man said, "Your category is technical. Step outside, please."

Grayson did not budge. He had scarcely heard what his guide said, in the sense that the words made only the smallest meaning for him. What he did hear was "outside." *Step outside!* But, he argued the point entirely inside his own head, outside is 2600 feet up. He could—he told himself—step from inside of the elevator to the inside of what was beyond the elevator door.

And, of course, there was a certain flexibility of thought whereby it was possible for one to be outside of a specific inside without having to be on the surface of a planet with only the sky above.

He came to that reluctant conclusion. And realized what the real problem was.

The real problem was that he didn't want to step out of the elevator, and into this below-ground universe. His feeling was that if he walked through that door, and into the narrow little hallway, which was all that he could see from where he stood, he would (he believed) have a hard time ever getting back in again, either now or later, here or elsewhere.

"You coming with me?" he asked the man.

His guide shook his head, but said nothing. He motioned with his hand, pointed with his thumb, toward the open door.

Grayson went, because—he felt the truth of it deep into his groin—he wasn't emotionally prepared to offer resistance until (he told himself) he had had his interview with the Utt Commissioner.

He took altogether five steps, and then he was "outside." Involuntarily, because he still *needed* the elevator, he turned, had a fleeting glimpse of a sort of an anteroom toward which the corridor he was in led; and then, because what was there slowed his turn and caught his attention, he delayed his about-face until the exact instant that the door clicked shut. The light in the elevator was vaguely visible through the translucent material of which the machine was made. As Grayson stood there, that light moved up, and out of his sight; and was gone. And he was alone.

Well, not entirely. In that brief glimpse he had had of the anteroom down here, he had had a swift impression of a young woman sitting behind, or in, some kind of a booth.

The sight of her brought a mental picture of a live human female reporting for work every morning at this reception desk; and then at night taking the elevator to the surface, and going about her private affairs like any office worker off duty. . . . One thing, only, wrong with that thought. How come there was no grapevine from such people about such an underground world?

Close up—after he had walked over to her—her presence down here was distinctly less reassuring. She was older, close up. Her cheeks had an unhealthy pallor to them; her brown eyes were dull, and, when she spoke, it was in an apathetic voice. "What's your category?" she asked.

Grayson remembered what his guide had said. So he replied, "Technical."

He placed his summons on her desk. But she ignored it, and instead looked down at an open ledger she had. "Name?" she asked.

Grayson gave it. But he had an unusual thought: Was it possible that this woman lived down here? Had she spent her adult existence at this remote distance from the sun? For the period of that thought, and of the feeling that came with it, he had a return of what could only be described as *responsibility*.

It was with the resultant voice of power that he said, "How long have you been down here?"

Even in his own ears, his tone had total authority in it. As if the Leader of the Country or the President of the Company had accidentally discovered an injustice in some cubbyhole of his domain. And he *always* corrected injustice when he became aware of it; he was that kind of a person. Under such circumstances, the individual addressed understood that somebody like God had heard his prayers and that He Who Could Act was standing here prepared to make a complete amend.

The effect upon the woman was electrifying. Tears came to her eyes. "Eighteen years, sir. Oh, please help me."

Having spoken, she dissolved into a mad crying. Other words gurgled out of her, but Grayson could not identify a single additional meaning. Since it was information he wanted, the tall, gaunt man reached across the desk with probing fingers and took hold of the woman's shoulder. And realized it was already too late. There was something about the way she now held herself, and about the increasing, spasmodic nature of her crying that signaled a message of change coming. She was starting to think again—that was the message. And to realize what she had done. And to be appalled.

Abruptly, the first overt reaction took place. She drew back. "I beg your pardon," she half-sobbed, "I haven't been feeling very well lately."

What she said was entirely understandable. A progressively anxious Grayson, fearing additional withdrawal before he learned further details, said quickly, "In that eighteen years, have you been allowed to go to the surface?"

A pair of swollen, slightly bloodshot eyes stared at him. And there was no question: she was regaining control. As he watched, helpless, her lips tightened. "You must forgive me," she gulped. "It is really disgraceful of me to show my unwell condition in public."

She was escaping him. Grayson made one more verbal grab. "Perhaps I can help you," he said urgently. "Tell me what your situation is. Do you live down here?"

She must have had a thought, then. For several moments longer, the original feeling must have come back; the feeling that he might actually be able to do what his words said. For she hesitated.

Into that hesitation, Grayson projected: "How old were you when you were brought down here? How was it done? What were the circumstances?"

But it was—he saw—too late. The woman's lips tightened. "Why are you asking me these personal questions?" she said.

"You requested me," said Grayson, gazing directly into her eyes, "to help you."

"I suddenly felt ill," was the reply.

No question she was recovering rapidly. Grayson said quickly, "You told me you had been imprisoned down here eighteen years."

"I don't remember making such a statement." Her

face was tense, anxious now, as if she feared repercussions from her indiscretion.

Grayson had previously withdrawn his outstretched hand. Now, he stepped back, put his hand in his pocket, and pointed the direction finder. While he did so, he made his final effort to capture her. He said, "At some future time, when you discover that I could have helped you, remember you turned it down. Either you answer me truthfully now, or don't ever expect assistance."

She was visibly fully recovered. A faint, contemptuous smile crinkled those pale cheeks; in fact, there was even a touch of color in her face, as she said, "A man help a woman—don't be ridiculous."

She glanced down at the paper he had handed her. Her contempt deepened. "Oh," she said in a ridiculing tone, "you have an appointment with the Utt Commissioner." She began to laugh. "Imagine," she said scathingly, "someone that will never be heard from again talking such nonsense."

Grayson snatched at the opportunity. "It's only an interview," he prompted.

"Hah!" she said scornfully.

He had lost his advantage with her. But he decided it was a mistake to have made any threat at all.

"Forget what I said a moment ago—" He spoke gently. "If you ever need help, and I'm in a position to give it, you can count on me."

The woman did not reply to those words directly. Her arm and hand had come up, and were pointing. "Go through that door!" she said.

Without further resistance, Grayson went. His effort to obtain information from her had produced threatening data; but it was better than no data at all. He had a feeling that she had not in all the previous years she had been down here lost her professional calm. Achieving that much from the poor creature was a weak victory, but a victory.

What I've got to do, he thought, is brace myself, and decide about this interview, which will obviously go against me. So, as soon as I'm through that door, I'll—

He was actually opening "that" door by the time he was formulating his purpose to have a purpose. Firmly, he drew it wide, and stepped forward—

Chapter Fifteen

Grayson sighed, and turned over on the cot. And, simultaneously, became aware of about eight things.

First impression: he was in a room ten feet square and nine feet high. Impressions second, third, fourth, *et al,* followed rapidly: Brightly lighted room. At one end was a washbasin. Beside it, standing in the open, a toilet with a seat but no lid. And next to *it* was a shower stall without a shower curtain.

There was a flat panel indentation behind the washbasin. A small table stood against the wall opposite the bed, and a chair stood at one end of the table.

That was the entire collection of furnishings that he could see. No, one more item: a mirror above the basin.

He was lying fully dressed on a narrow bed against one wall of a room with translucent plastic walls and ceiling. From inside of each wall and from the entire ceiling, the brightness poured out and down into the room. Like a sunlit day; that was the effect. The floor was bare, marble-like, opaque, but it gleamed faintly in the brilliant light from every side.

As his roving gaze snatched first one piece of information and then another from those few visible items, he suddenly realized that for the entire minute or so he had been awake, he had been looking for something that he could not find.

Where's the door?

As he had that thought, he moved. In one awkward leap, he was off the bed. Two strides carried him to the logical place for a door to be: somewhere on the otherwise blank wall opposite the toilet, washbasin, and shower.

It was as he reached that wall, and began to run his fingers over it, searching, that a thought lightly touched the outer edge of his consciousness.

A dim memory—

There was enough emotional energy in that first recollection to soften the hard pressing of his fingers against the wall. Enough memory, presently, to cause him to turn around and, once more, with widened eyes, to survey the little room with its primitive furnishings.

—How did I get here . . . from there?

There, as he now recalled it, was his act of opening an extremely visible door, which the woman receptionist had indicated: *"Go through that door!"*

As he remembered the moment, and remembered pushing the door open, and realized that he had no recollection of any kind from then to now, the disturbed energy inside him expanded to a new intensity, and became—outrage.

So that was how an Utt Commissioner interrogated a human being! The sense of indignation was heightened almost to a frenzy by his realization, here and now, that he had been totally taken by surprise. He was still fumbling at the wall by the time he had that realization. But a remote part of his mind accepted that finding the entrance to this room was not going to be easy.

—This is my prison cell, he thought, suddenly grim.

Abruptly, he turned and walked back to the cot, and, as abruptly, sat down. Again, more minutely, he reviewed the events that had led from there to here. This time, he realized that he had, somehow, taken it for granted that the door through which the receptionist had directed him would lead to a corridor; and that he would have time to consider, and to plan, and to brace himself, and to activate those three—of the eleven —plastic inserts which were not automatic.

That thought was his first recollection of the inserts. Hastily, he fumbled at the places where he had put them, and—relief!—they were all still there.

At that instant, with that realization of not having lost everything, he experienced an utterly unexpected feeling:

Admiration for the Utt . . . It was a feeling he had never had before in his life. And it seemed so irrational that he found himself arguing against it. But it would not go away. . . . What a completely skillful thing they had done; that was the substance of his genuine congratulatory thought.

He presumed that, while he was unconscious, they had questioned him, and extracted what he knew about The Revolution, had gotten a confession of his affair with Miss Haskett, and of his own private schemes. While he was helpless, everything must have tumbled out of him.

—Know your enemy, he thought with a smile. They did. But he didn't.

Only one thing seemed unexplained: how come they had left him with his battery of inserts? It smacked of contempt. But, maybe—a hopeful possibility—they simply hadn't taken his defenses seriously. And so had not inquired about what *he* could do to help himself.

The idea had a certain plausibility, and buoyed him during the minutes that now went by; several of them. He was abruptly, once more, too restless to remain seated.

He tried the toilet. It flushed noisily, giving a stereotyped performance. The faucets in the shower produced an excellent stream of water. The mirror above the wash-basin turned out to be the door of a typical bathroom cabinet, complete with toiletry items, including shave cream and razor, comb and brush, and a sparkling-clean glass.

In the same matter-of-fact fashion, Grayson inspected the indented tabletop under the cabinet. It must have a purpose; in a room as small as this, everything would have been designed for practical utility. Persistent, curious, he was reaching across the basin and probing the wall beyond—when he accidentally caught a glimpse of his watch. He drew back, and stared at the timepiece.

Only sixteen minutes after eleven o'clock!

He fumbled his way back to the cot, and for a while his shock grew with each moment. He was—he realized —accepting that it was eleven-sixteen this same day-time. And that in slightly over one hour he had been removed from the planet earth as he knew it. Removed, also, from his fantasy of a victorious male living a peaceful, determined existence. And deposited in a tiny prison in what, in effect, was another universe.

Feeling overwhelmed—and temporarily without admiration—he lay back on the cot.

A thought came. There had to be an explanation, he told himself, for his blanking out *instantly* as he stepped through the door. Not even a bullet in the heart or through the head could knock out a human being—instantly.

Lying there, he considered the various possibilities. He rejected chemicals, because there was really only one way in which consciousness could be blotted out at the speed of light, and that was at the speed of thought: a certain stage of hypnotism.

But—Grayson argued with himself—that way would have required previous contact, and total—but total —trance. The absolute deepest stage: the somnam-bulistic stage beyond visual and auditory hallucinations.

When, how, under what circumstances could that have been induced?

Slowly, as he reasoned about that, admiration returned. And what was especially convincing about his analysis was that when he triggered the relevant insert, and the counter-hypnotic chemical was injected into his blood, he could feel the freeing response.

At once, he was brighter. An enormous confidence surged, and the thought:—I have no further business in this sub-world.

The problem (he realized) would be to get out of this room. Nothing he could do until that was achieved.

He lay back. And waited.

Chapter Sixteen

At twelve-thirty sharp, there was a faint sound from the panel above the sink. Grayson sat up, put his feet on the floor, and watched as the panel slid back. At once, he was his usual alert self. Thus, he had a perceptive, fleeting glimpse of an opening. It was visible literally for moments only.

During those moments, three cartons slid onto the mysterious tabletop, which was recessed into the wall behind the sink. Grayson climbed to his feet, went over, and opened the containers. As he had swiftly suspected, they were his lunch: a hot liquid of some kind—tea, it turned out—in one carton, two meat sandwiches in another, and a dish of pudding with a creamer package in the third.

Well—he was resigned—so now he knew how lunch and, most likely, dinner and breakfast were presented to the prisoners on an individual basis, without their ever leaving their rooms. Grayson sniffed at the sandwiches and the tea, and later at the pudding. He decided they were not poisoned, and ate everything. While he did so, he thought again of the problem of escape.

And once more found himself with a single possibility:

Wait!

He waited all afternoon. At six, a chicken dinner with mashed potatoes, peas, red currant jelly, coffee, and a piece of apple pie with ice cream emerged from the panel under the mirror. Four cartons contained the sumptuous repast.

He ate, drank, and sincerely commended the Utt for their comprehension of the human appetite. And then, since there was nothing else to do—back to the bed.

He was still lying there when a hidden bell rang. Grayson rolled over on the cot, saw by his watch that it was seven o'clock, and simultaneously strove to identify where the ringing came from. Unfortunately, locating a sound was one thing he had never been good at. The ringing ceased before he could decide its origin.

Several moments went by, and then a woman's voice said, "At seven-thirty an exit for your room will be available. If you wish to attend the weekly community meeting, use the exit and follow the arrows to your nearest community room."

If he wished to attend—

By the time the message completed, Grayson was sitting up, guessing that there was a speaker behind *each* wall. While he waited for the thirty minutes to pass, he showered, utilized the toiletries in the cabinet above the sink to shave his beard-darkened face, and combed his straight, brown hair. Several minutes before the half-hour, he was sitting on his cot, fully dressed, looking his usual gaunt, plain self. But he was on edge, as tense as he could be, and as spruced up as was possible for him.

Exactly on the half-hour, there was a click. And then—

An opening appeared in the ceiling. Narrow steps folded down through it to the floor. Grayson leaped awkwardly forward and grabbed at the tough, plastic structure. He held on firmly, while he peered up at what seemed to be other walls. What was up there gleamed as if it, also, was lighted from a hidden source. Was it a corridor up there? he wondered.

He climbed hastily, almost missing his footing a couple of times in his eagerness. But he made it. And it was, indeed, a corridor. His entrance to it was protected by a guard rail, which projected a good three feet above the floor.

There was a small sign on the fence. It said in large letters:

REMEMBER
Your Room Number Is 231 in Corridor G

Below that in smaller print were the words:

> Occupant must be back in his quarters by midnight exactly. Failure to comply involves a penalty.

Grayson wrote the number down. But his thought actually was: —I'm not coming back this way. So, goodbye, little room.

And he meant *little*.

He was standing erect now. All along the corridor, he could see other fences, similar to the one that enclosed his little stairway. More entrances, he presumed.

What an amazing prison. It must have cost a fortune to install. But, of course, the Utt government had the whole human economy under its control. And so enough money was available for maintenance of its enforcement system. And, presumably, enough human beings to do all the work of maintaining.

It was, he realized, those human employees of the Utt who interested him . . . first, above everything else. What was the administrative structure? Who was in charge? How many individuals were involved? Since power and control were at stake, there would be a hierarchy with a strong interest in having the Utt takeover of earth continue indefinitely.

The Utt themselves seemed to be a rather peaceful, well-meaning race. But—Grayson had no doubt—their human underlings would kill to retain their ascendancy.

So—careful! But finding out who they were had to be his initial goal. So it seemed to Grayson.

Even as his mind hardened on that purpose, he discovered that the arrows (which the woman's voice had mentioned) were arrow-shaped lights in the floor. He was briskly following them, when all along the corridor, human heads began to show through the long line of guard rails.

Men came up out of the openings. A few. Then, as he turned a corner, a dozen . . . many . . . too numerous to count easily. Scores. Grayson found himself walking half a stride behind a sturdy, pale-faced man of about thirty-five, who did not glance at him, or show awareness of any of the other men. In fact, as far as Grayson could determine, nobody looked at anyone. There was no sign of people recognizing each other. And no one spoke. Except for the clicking of many shoes, it was a long, silent parade that steadily increased in numbers. It seemed to know where it was going. And just about the time that Grayson estimated that he had gone a quarter of a mile, he saw that the men in the distance ahead of him were turning leftward through an open doorway from which a bright light shone.

Grayson, approaching the entrance a minute later, thought: So he now had a partial picture of this underground world. It consisted of men. They were imprisoned all day, and maybe all week, in little ten-by-ten rooms. And once every seven days they emerged to participate in—what?

That, it seemed to him, was something he should find out before he departed this network of human-built caves.

Bare moments after that thought, and that renewed decision, he himself made the left turn, and saw the "what" that was there with his own eyes.

What he saw was an anteroom, ornately decorated like a theater lobby, and brightly lighted by chandeliers that hung from a surprisingly high-domed ceiling. As in a theater, there were several sets of double doors that—as Grayson entered the anteroom—were all momentarily opening and shutting. What seemed to be a large, darkened room was partly visible through one of the doors as it was opened, in turn, by the next four men, of whom two had been ahead of him, and two behind.

A theater?—Grayson wondered.

He had stepped to one side, uncertain. As he hesitated three more men opened one or other of the double doors, and entered. And each opening there was the same impression of a large, dark area.

—At least, I should go in and look around. . . .

It was decision. Moments later, as he slipped through from the brightness to the dimness, his first, earlier impression also became his second: *Could it be a theater?*

Wholly inside, Grayson paused to look around. It took a little while to accustom himself to the dimness. And even after he could see, it was difficult to make out the faces of the men around him; even those nearest were a blur. Which, to begin with, greatly relieved him. Because, if he couldn't see them, then they couldn't see him any better. The distant stage, of which he presently became aware, was equally dimly lit. Except that behind it, or rather slightly off to one side, was a . . . reflection (not a direct view) . . . of greater brightness beyond some barrier.

Stronger than before, and more purposefully, came the thought: This has got to be my only visit here. . . . His feeling: all I need is a quick look around. Get an idea of the place. And then return to the surface.

Going back to his room, and letting himself be locked up again, would be a total waste of time. He was a man who was bracing for battle with a race that had conquered earth, and had then—he believed—departed. Nothing to be gained by an extended imprisonment in the bowels of the earth—so it seemed to Peter Grayson.

Around him, as he had these thoughts, men were

talking. The murmur of voices was a strangely subdued sound for so large a room, and (now that his eyes were even more accustomed to the dimness) it seemed an especially subdued noise because *so many* individuals were doing the talking.

Evidently, there was a rule: no conversation in the corridors. But talking could be done here, in an undertone, in that almost whisper known as *sotto voce*.

He had been hesitating as the numerous impingements came in upon his eyes and ears. And now he consciously suppressed an impulse to ask one of the men about the bright area near the stage. The truth was that he should go and look for himself. The rationale of that was: The fact is, there are no Utt on earth. They came. They did their good deed. And they departed, leaving behind a human maintenance crew to enforce their solution to earth's problems.

From now on, it would be his quiet task to search out that maintenance crew. And first of all find out how they operated. Then decide what to do about them.

At this stage that meant no one must suspect him. Therefore, no questions. No introductions if he could help it. And of course it would be ridiculous if he left this place without a minimum investigation of anything mysterious. Like the lighted area.

With that determination, noting that the stage was a hundred yards away, he began to push in that direction. What he came to was metal wall. Metal—not stone, not concrete, or wood. It felt more than just solid. His fingertips, accustomed to so many sensitivities, experienced the feel of an unusually heavy metal. Not just the smoothness of steel, or brass, or even good iron. As he walked beside it, he kept those fingertips running over the heavy, solid wall. And the closer he got to where the light came through, the more puzzled he felt.

It was an almost blank puzzlement. Because he couldn't quite accept the interpretation of the solidness that his brain fed back to him. Lead? Here? For what?

It was a few seconds after that when he came to

the light source. It was a glass door; and the light streamed through it. It was a much brighter light than it had appeared to be from a distance. Grayson noticed at once what was causing the dimming effect. The light shone against the dark curtains that hung down from the stage. And that was where the reflection came from.

He forgot that; because there was lettering on the glass. Yellow tinted letters that spelled out virtually meaningless words:

ENTRANCE TO HELL
HOME OF THE DEVIL
STAY OUT

Something about the "glass" had already attracted Grayson's expert attention. Tentatively, he ran his fingers over the transparent substance. Instant astonishment. Again, the feel was of solid, heavy metal.

Finally, now, he pressed his face against the substance. And peered in. After a long moment, a frown came. And puzzlement.

What he was looking into was, first of all, a tunnel. Beyond that was a surprisingly large room. And in the center of the room, about fifty feet from the entrance, was what looked like thousands of small flickering fires in an intricate configuration.

A baffled Grayson studied the "fires." There was something about them . . . not just strange. He had seen many models in his time: representations of bits and pieces of matter or energy. Some of them had been merely interesting. Some had been startling—brilliantly conceived. And a few he recalled as having been sensational. This one was sensational.

Could it be a model of . . . the interior of a sun?

Automatically, he fumbled for the latch, intending to go in for a closer inspection, when—a man's voice said, "I wouldn't go in, sir."

The voice came from the shadows at the far side of the door. The speaker was hard to see because the brightness coming through the door had a blinding effect. But, after a few moments, Grayson was able to make out a middle-aged—fortyish—man, neatly dressed in a brown suit. Businessman type—he guessed.

The man spoke again, in an explaining tone: "That fire flares out at uneven intervals. And several persons who were put in there were burned to a cinder by a single flare."

The scientist Grayson had an immediate thought about that. "This flare! When it comes, does it seem to move very slowly?"

The other man's blue eyes widened. "Hey," he said, "you've seen an execution?" He added, with a frown, "I don't remember seeing you before."

So they were going to have to go through that routine. Patiently, Grayson explained that his training was in physics, and that this was his first day in the underground.

His information evoked another diversion. "Let me introduce myself," said his new acquaintance. "I'm Herb Lartmore. Something happened in my vision situation. Got my wife completely under control. Ran my own business, though legally, of course, she owned it, and could take over anytime. In spite of that, some damned female acquaintance of hers reported me. And here I've been now for four years." Once again, he had an afterthought: "I've sort of taken on the job of guarding this door. What's your story?"

"Well," said Grayson, "something happened to my vision, also. I reported it to my ophthalmologist. And here I am."

"You nut!" said the man. But his tone was friendly.

In the silence that followed, Grayson remembered the grim realities. He said, "You say men have been deliberately put in there, and burned. Put in by whom?"

The reply was: "The powers that be." A shrug. "About a dozen armed men have several times come in here during our weekly community meet. Each time they drag in one person, bring him over here, open the door, and shove him inside. Then they stand here, and wait for the flare to kill him."

"And the executed person is actually burned to a cinder?" Grayson asked.

"It's instantaneous," was the reply. Tears came suddenly to his eyes. "I remember one poor guy. He was screaming—"

"These victims," Grayson persisted, "do they belong to our group?"

The man who had identified himself as Herb Lartmore was shaking his head. "In my four years I've pretty well got to recognize everybody, so I notice the new people as they come in—" He broke off. "My guess is that it's one of the maintenance people who's broken discipline. And the Utt evidently allow no mercy for such."

Deliberately, Grayson turned and looked again through the transparent metal into "hell." The labeling of the place with such a stereotype was undoubtedly intended to have significance. Though it was not easy to decide what.

Here was a hell never dreamed of by the denizens of ancient Galilee. . . . For God's sake, he thought, it's got to be a model. The real thing would be multimillions of degrees hot in Fahrenheit or Centigrade, and the radiation alone would require many feet of lead— which they've got. . . . But the fact was, with such temperatures the lead would melt, unless—

The "unless" did its inexorable things inside his knowledgeable head. The key factor was the kind of stability that would be mandatory inside the central mass of a certain type of blue sun.

Accordingly, this that he was seeing could be an actual interior of that kind of super-hot blue sun. By some magic of Utt super-science that incredible cross-section was being held in juxtaposition to this area of space and time. The faraway sun balanced itself where it was, and only an occasional flare reached out and through as that balance was fleetingly disturbed.

He was backing away. "Uh, I'll be talking to you again, Herb. Uh, good luck."

"Whatever that means," was the bitter-tone reply.

Grayson had turned away. In his anxiety to be away, he did not look back at the self-appointed guardian of the gate to hell.

His journey to the distant entrance cost him the same hassle as before. Except that now he was more frantic, less patient. Inside him was a stronge rage, and the thought: If I ever meet up with those maintenance people, I'll—

It was not exactly clear in that overheated emotional moment what he would do. And so he was still raging about it as he emerged into the bright foyer, and started for the hall doorway by which he had originally entered the place.

Chapter Seventeen

What really distracted him, then, was that men were still coming in from that self-same corridor. Which would seem to imply that the main entertainment of the evening had not yet begun.

As he slowed, Grayson became aware of three youthful-looking males standing slightly off to one side. He had time to notice that he was the only one coming out. And time, also, to hope that spies from the in-group might observe that fact, also.

He actually veered toward them before he realized that they had been standing, scanning the arrivals; and that their attention had concentrated completely on him.

With that, he came to a full stop. He was marginally aware that other men were entering from the corridor, and walking to the various sets of double doors. He was even vaguely conscious that not a single one of the arrivals paid heed to the drama of himself and the three young men.

The three came forward as a group, separating as

they came up. One stepped in front of him, and the other two behind.

It was these latter two who grabbed him.

For Grayson, there was a sense of everything happening slowly. His instant feeling was that he wanted them to succeed, and wanted them to take him to wherever they had in mind. To that end, he did not resist; lifted not a finger, did not brace himself, tightened not a single muscle.

The men seemed not to notice that they had a willing prisoner. The two who held him jerked him roughly; twisted his arms. And the knee of one of them came up and jabbed hard into the small of his back.

In this painful fashion they held Grayson, while the third man put a gag in his mouth. He did it with a wolf-ish smile, and strong, brutal fingers. Grayson's head was snapped back. He felt a sharp ache in his neck. The gag seemed huge, and he could hardly breathe.

He was appalled. The feeling came that he was only a single muscular twist away from death. And what was suddenly massively astonishing was that, *still* no one paid any attention. It was a vague awareness at fringe level of perception. The men were still coming in from the corridor. And they didn't look; they didn't react.

His captors were tying his hands now. The cord they used was thin and strong. It bit deep into his skin, cutting off circulation. Sensing the potential disaster of that, Grayson slightly expanded his lower arm muscles. So far as he could make out, then, they didn't notice. Because when his wrists were finally bound, and the effort and violence of the tying ceased, he was able to relax the tightened muscles; and the cord didn't seem all that binding.

Not that he had much time to evaluate the situation. They were walking him rapidly to the door. It was a case of finding a moment when no one was coming in. But they seemed to know the rhythm of this under-ground universe. They reached the door, and stopped. A man entered. The three men, almost as if they re-acted to a hidden timer, snapped Grayson and themselves through the opening, across the threshold, and out into the corridor.

What seemed to be no more than a split instant later, the next male zombie came opposite the door, turned, and entered. And *he* did not look at Grayson or at the men who now spun the physicist around, and *ran* him farther along the corridor.

A faster-than-trot run, it was, for about a hundred yards straight ahead; then, a sharp, almost skidding turn around a corner, and along that corridor about two dozen feet—and stop. Grayson, breathing hard, saw that they were in front of a door. One of the men reached forward—casually after so much dynamic movement—and knocked unhurriedly.

The door opened—on pitch darkness.

He had a blank moment of contemplating that. And then he was jostled from behind. A signal to move? He presumed it to be so, and thereupon walked through the open doorway as if it were his own decision.

The momentary sense of freedom to act . . . ended. A pair of hands that he did not see, but whose owner evidently saw him, came out of the darkness and grabbed him. They were strong, and he was pliable. They propelled him across what felt like a carpeted floor, and then abruptly stopped him. As he was held upright, something hard shoved forcibly into his knees from behind. A chair?—he wondered. The hands pushed him down—hard. And, yes, it was a chair.

As the shock of so much handling faded, Grayson leaned back tentatively. And was relieved to find that he was sitting in a chair that did, in fact, have a back-rest.

Out of the darkness, a familiar voice said, "Well, Doctor, here we are again."

It was the voice of The Revolution.

Grayson continued to sit. The darkness remained unrelieved. Yet he realized he did not so much feel threatened as disappointed.

There had been a hope in him that he was in the hands of somebody who ran things for the Utt. Instead

—the same group of rebels . . . Basically, they were people who, like himself, were presumably in their own more determined fashion seeking to penetrate the same mystery.

Sighing inwardly, Grayson waited. He anticipated that he would now be verbally pummeled and shoved and degraded. But there was also a hope that the end result would be another droplet or two of information.

The first thing that happened was a surprise. Out of the darkness came another pair of hands. Fingers touched the knot at the back of his neck, and, amazingly, began to loosen it. It came free. And his mouth was free of the gag, free to open and shut, and free, undoubtedly, to talk.

But he said nothing. Simply waited.

As he sat there, a faint light began to glow from a recess in the center of the table in front of which—he now discovered—he was sitting. The light pointed up slantwise at the face and shoulders of a large man who sat across the table from him. The rest of the room remained night-wrapped, its other inhabitants invisible from where he sat.

The other man's face was only marginally familiar to Grayson. Without his woman's clothing and woman's hair, the leader of The Revolution looked like a puffy-faced, heavyset male. Though he wore a shirt and tie, he had the appearance of a truck driver on his day off.

. . . Interesting that he was willing to reveal his true appearance. It had an all-outness to it, as if he were taking a final gamble. Grayson, thinking about that, felt a shaking start inside him.

Life or death—he decided—in the next few minutes.

What astonished him presently was that he was not really afraid. With that awareness the shaking ceased. It was actually just a reaction to a memory of past fears—and to hell with that!

He sat there, and he saw by the light from the table that the big man's eyes were steely gray. They seemed to be focused on something that he held in his hands.

The hands came up into the spotlight. Grayson saw that they held a pair of eyeglasses.

"Take a look at these specs," said the big man.

He held them out as if he anticipated that Grayson would reach forward and take them. There was a pause. Abruptly, he seemed to realize. "Uh!" he said. He shrugged. "Well," he continued tolerantly, "it would be inadvisable to untie a man who was able to locate our headquarters, walk into it, and leave it. So I'll just hold these up close to you."

As the spectacles were pushed up to within inches of his eyes, Grayson peered at them. And then peered some more as the holding fingers turned them over. They were—he could see—a pair of expensive frames with skillfully manufactured lens. Nothing cheap here. These were the best, like his own.

All right. So his captor had an effective pair of spectacles. So?

He must have made a dismissing, or a negating, facial gesture. The big man said sharply, "Look closer!"

It wasn't so much, then, that Grayson looked closer as that he looked *again*. And this time he saw what he was expected to: a fine, transparent tape was affixed on each of the lenses.

Good God, could it be?—

"Yes," said the voice softly, "it's the tape put out for scientific uses by the Haskett Manufacturing Laboratories. *It's* what does the job of nullifying what the Utt glasses do."

"B-but—" stammered Grayson, "that means—" He couldn't go on. The complications seemed too far reaching, seemed to mean that the entire problem of malekind was simply resolvable. Every man would buy the sticky tape he had invented for Haskett Laboratories and himself privately glue it over the lenses of his glasses.

Or was there some reason why that was not the solution?

What instantly bothered Grayson was that he had clearly been given key information. And he couldn't really think of why, with such an obvious method available, they had bothered with Peter Grayson as an individual. . . .

Stronger than before came the feeling: life or death.

Grayson had leaned forward to examine the spectacles. Now, he settled back again. And there he was aware once more of the darkness all around—except for that single spotlight focused on The Revolution.

Was there anyone else in the room? Startling to realize that he did not know if the three men who had captured him had come inside with him.

Since he hadn't heard the door open or seen a resultant light from the corridor, the man who had removed his gag must still be nearby. But it did seem to Grayson that he could hear the slow breathing of more than one person.

—Should I try to get out of this situation? he asked himself. . . . The silent question was a tentative attempt at having a purpose of his own. But he realized immediately that at this stage it was foolish to think in such terms. Even if he were successful, it would leave him tied hand and foot. Then what would he do?

Besides, the truth was, he was curious. Explanations, it seemed to him, were in order. Before anything else. So why not start in that roundabout way?

Quickly, he explained about the blond man, who had surprised him in the dark at Haskett Laboratories, and had tried to kill him. "Was that," he asked, "one of your strong-arm boys?"

"Yep." The Revolution nodded. "And you kind've had me worried there, Doc. You almost lost out in that situation to one guy."

Grayson waited. He had a feeling he was missing something. But that he had better not volunteer astonishment. He could, personally, see nothing disgraceful about an older man suffering defeat in hand-to-hand combat with a powerfully built younger man.

The Revolution continued in that same dark tone. "What still bothers me," he said, "is that, according to the report I got, you won against that attack by just plain muscle power."

Grayson had a picture, now, of a man who required scientific defenses from a doctor of physics. "The moment we grappled," he parried that expectation, "I realized he hadn't been doing his push-ups like he should. So it was a good workout for somebody like me who had."

Silence. Then, grudgingly: "I guess that's a good answer. But you'll have to do better than that in this situation, Doc. So, get ready!"

. . . All right, thought Grayson, wearily, all right. So I'd better show I'm still alive, and have a brain—perhaps, it was time for less permissiveness and more aggressiveness.

"What do you want?" he said, curtly.

The face in front of him remained impassive for several seconds after those words were spoken. Then, the eyes blinked. Next, the lips parted. Excitement rippled across the face. Finally:

"Hey!" said the man. "What's that tone I hear in your voice? Power? Where did that come from?"

Grayson merely continued to stare at the other. There was no reaction he could think of making.

"Doc," went on the voice urgently, "we need a leader who understands science as good as you do. We've got the organization, but we don't know how to use it."

A thought came. Grayson said, "You seem to manage pretty well. How much of this sub-world do you control?"

The face in the light twisted into a wolfish smile. "The Utt," said the man, "operate like automatons. They set up a system, and so long as you don't interfere with that system, they don't notice."

"The system seems to have a lot of holes in it if you can come down here at will," said Grayson.

"It *has* a lot of holes in it. I *can* come down here at will."

"Then if I agree to do what you want, you'll get me out of here?"

The moment he had spoken, Grayson realized he had said the wrong thing.

"Doc," came the voice, suddenly soft in an unreassuring way, "if you can't get yourself out of here, we don't want you."

Grayson was silently, grimly, critical of himself for having precipitated the crisis. But it also seemed to him that there was no immediate turning back. "The existence of this underground world caught me by surprise," he said defensively. It seemed to him that he could not possibly make any other admission or statement because that might be exactly what they wanted from him. "So"—he finished unhappily—"I'll need your help on that."

"If that's your answer," was the suddenly cold reply, "then we don't need to continue this conversation." The heavily jowled face was abruptly gloomy. The thick lips parted and said savagely, "You may recall, Doctor, I told you that if I ever had a bad feeling about you— *Kaput!*"

He raised his voice. "Okay, Hal, kill him!"

Chapter Eighteen

Grayson shifted position slightly in his chair, and moved his bound hands—slightly. Then he held his breath, and started counting.

In front of him, the big man slumped down on the table, and crouched there limply, face down, arms sprawled.

Behind Grayson, there were thud sounds.

He continued counting to ninety—which was the safety margin—and then went on to a hundred to make absolutely sure.

And then he gasped for air.

He sat for at least a minute, breathing hard. When he finally stood up gingerly, it was with an unhappy feeling of: "Surely, it's not going to be that easy. Surely, The Revolution took such possibilities into account, and has a second line of defense."

The moments went by and became a minute. And that minute lengthened to another; and still there was no sign.

While he waited for the counter-strike that never

came, it seemed to Grayson that the floor felt uneven to his feet. Swiftly, he saw the problem. A man whose hands were tied behind his back could not balance himself properly. And so—careful!

Nonetheless, he was quickly hopeful. And when he finally moved it was on the basis that, except for his bound hands, he had achieved complete victory.

Crouching, kneeling, sitting, bending, and cursing under his breath, he now tried to insert his fingers into various pockets. First, he searched the big man, then the four individuals who lay on the floor each in his own twisted position. The final, though horribly delayed, result was not bad. He found the knife he craved —a switchblade that jumped into ready position at the touch of a button. But he found it after nearly thirty minutes. And found it in what was probably the second or third last pocket of the fifth man he tackled.

Which fitted, he thought with the bitterness of exhaustion. He had always believed that, if such a thing as ESP or luck existed, his supply was exactly zero. Which had been one of the reasons why science had been, and was still, such a haven for him. He needed systematic thoughts for the totally missing intuition.

Even as he had those strong feelings of frustration, the knife was doing its freeing action.

The instant he was free, he was, to his surprise, no longer a man in a hurry. Up to the exact moment that the thin cord fell away from his wrists, his instinct had been to get out of this room right now.

The feeling faded. The impulse to escape yielded to a practical consideration: —I've got these people here. They'll be unconscious for another half-hour. Why don't I search them. . . ?

Particularly, then, he removed the contents of the pockets of the big man. Grayson was amazed to realize that he was completely calm and completely remorseless. The other's command to a henchman to kill him canceled all obligation he had ever had to The Revolution.

There was no time to examine his "take." He simply

stuffed likely looking items into his pockets, and discarded handkerchiefs, pens, money, empty billfolds, keys, four automatics (but he removed their bullets), and a variety of obvious nothings. What he kept were notebooks, unidentifiable devices, the special pair of spectacles, one automatic, and all the cartridges.

Moments after that he was out in the hallway; and it was, he decided, not the time to investigate the zombie types in the "community" room.

There were other more important things to do.

It was twenty-eight minutes later. He stood at a doorway. The tingle in his arm said that he was close to his destination.

In his mind was a kind of desolate memory of a dozen deserted corridors, and long, blank, brightly lighted walls—the same inside-the-wall lighting effect. And in his body was a conscious bracing of his muscles with the intent of opening the doorway and stepping through into what he firmly believed was the reception area. His expectation included the elevators, and included also what had been purported to be the entrance to the Utt Commissioner's office.

He had several very simple, pure purposes. They all added up to the one idea: find out what was going on, and who these people were, and leave.

Okay! he thought grimly, and pushed the door open.

A bedroom. That was his first, mildly disappointed impression. With a woman in it.

Grayson didn't see the woman for several seconds. Accordingly, he had time to have a second reaction to the room . . . not a bedroom, but simply a variation on the ten-by-ten-by-ten box in which he himself had spent most of the day.

He was noticing that the variations consisted of drapery, a shower curtain, several small items of furniture, including a TV, a bookcase, and a rocking chair.

The rocking chair faced away from him. And it was in it that the woman sat, almost hidden by the high back.

She must have heard the door open, but not realized

what the sound was. Because she merely turned her head, casually, and glanced toward the door. And, of course—as it turned out—that was the same as a glance at Grayson.

Her eyes widened, and face twisted. Her body seemed to contort as she awkwardly scrambled to her feet, and sort of spun around.

She wore a long, silken nightdress, which was extremely filmy; her nude body was visible through it. And she had on slippers. In those first instants she obviously saw that it was a human male wearing glasses. This obviousness showed on her face, which took on a severe expression of censure. The same critical attitude showed in her body, which stiffened with the beginning of outrage.

The outrage was in her voice, as she said in the strident, censorious tone of an old-maid schoolteacher speaking to a little boy student: "What are you doing here? Men are not allowed in this section."

Belatedly, Grayson recognized the receptionist who had been behind the "basement" reception desk that morning. He chided himself: —Naturally, who else could it be . . . ? After all, it was she upon whom he had focused his detection device. And what was ridiculous about the present situation was that, somehow, he had taken it for granted that she would still be in the office.

He realized that the woman was having her own delayed recognition of him. "You're that man . . ."—she spoke accusingly—". . . this morning . . ."

For twenty-eight minutes he had been thinking what he would do at this moment of confrontation. Of the several possibilities, he now chose the most direct. With a deliberate sweep of his left hand, he removed his glasses.

For him, the room blurred. The female figure in front of him was abruptly less substantial. Misty. Details obscured. Her face changed into a blob.

Theoretically, she should have guessed that that would be his condition. But, of course, he had already discovered that people were not really aware. Here, also. According to his dim eyesight, during a long moment there was no visible reaction by the woman. Then:

"What do you want me to do?" It was a trembling voice that spoke the words. "Do you want me to take off my nightdress and lie down?" An almost whimper followed in an undertone: "Don't hurt me."

He had been intent. All day his insides had seemed to be continuously squeezed. And there had not been for a single moment an impulse toward feminine companionship, intimate or otherwise. It actually cost him an effort, now, to think about what might happen if he refused—which was his automatic impulse.

The instant question was: Did he have to do here what he had done the previous night to get the key from Miss Haskett? In short, was this another purchase situation?

He was unfortunately having some adverse personal recollections about his particular female. He found himself remembering her nasty attitude after she recovered from her emotional seizure twelve long hours before.

Having had that memory, it was suddenly easier to decide that no transaction was necessary.

With that, he realized what his purpose had to be. "Get dressed!" he commanded, curtly.

There was a pause. Then the woman said timidly, "You mean, in front of you, get dressed?"

It required simple, direct emotion to straighten that out. Grayson was not in the mood for illogical behavior. . . . One minute she offers to lie down naked; the next she's suddenly modest— Besides, he wouldn't be able to see her clearly, no matter what she did.

"Get dressed!" he snarled. "And quickly."

He was slightly amazed to realize, as he looked at her nude body a minute later—looked blurrily, it was true, but still she was visible—that she appeared to have a good figure. And her skin, as seen by his near-sighted eyes from a distance of six feet, seemed clear and unblemished.

He noted, idly, that she put on the same outfit which

she had worn that morning. When she was completely dressed, he pointed. "Go ahead of me!" he said. "And take me to the elevators."

The woman had started to move on his first words. But as he named the destination, she stopped. "I can't get in there at this hour," she said. "All the doors between here and there are locked until eight o'clock tomorrow morning. And besides"—her voice sank—"I pressed the alarm button when I went over to the sink. Somebody will be coming in a minute." She finished with a mumbled "I'm sorry."

"Nevertheless," said Grayson, "let's go toward the elevators." He followed her out of her room, and walked beside her. "What is your name?" he asked.

It was Nora Patton.

Grayson had his glasses back on. And so, with one eye, so to speak, on the corridor ahead, and another on the corridor to the rear, he spoke to her, seeking information.

"Have you ever been on the surface since being brought down here?"

"No."

"Not for eighteen years?"

"Eighteen." She nodded. She seemed suddenly apathetic, as if the mere turning of her thought to such details overwhelmed her spirit. Her face, which had a pretty shape, lost some of its color. Her eyes, when he looked down at them, had become dull. She said listlessly, "I'm not supposed to talk about such things."

"Who told you not to talk?"

"The woman upstairs."

"Does she come down here for the night?"

"Yes."

"Do the men I saw also live down here—the man who brought me down the elevator?"

"Yes."

"Do you associate with them?"

"No." Her voice quickened. "They have to get authorization, and the electric lock system has to be opened from a central control area for them to come in here."

"Who gives the authorization?"

"I don't know. It's a voice that speaks."

"A man's voice, or a woman's?"

"I'm not sure. It's a high tenor, or a low contralto."

"What happens when the authorization is given?"

"The doors unlock. Then they can get through."

"Who?"

"Oh, there're about a hundred men in the men's section."

Grayson ceased his questions. They had come to a door that looked metallic. He reached forward tentatively and touched it. It felt metallic, and solid. Steel? he wondered. Whatever, it was very convincing. And gave instant credence to what Nora Patton had said about not being able to enter the reception room except by permission.

Pity came. Mentally, he pictured the life these captured workers were living, and braced himself. All right, all right, he thought, so it's up to me.

Exactly why he should take responsibility was not entirely clear. Something to do, of course, with being threatened by the same trap. But also there was the fact that the thought had finally been presented to him. And so what he had never before considered in any way became an accepted assignment.

He stepped closer to the door. Pretended to press against it, as if he were testing it. Thus, he was able to rub the concealed device in his palm over the surface near what he believed to be the lock area. He had his ear against the metal, and, as he listened intently, the sound that he was waiting for came: a sharp click.

It was loud enough to have been easily audible, requiring no special attention. Still, you could never know about such matters in advance. It might have been a soft, oiled, sliding hiss of a sound.

Grayson could not help wondering if, perhaps, Nora had not led him to a pre-selected door. In her enslaved state, betrayal was mandatory. If so, then behind the door was a trap.

He could not, he realized, let the possibility make any difference.

Bracing himself, he grasped the woman's wrist firmly with his left hand. With his right he pressed the latch, which he had so swiftly and expertly unlocked. And pushed.

Emptiness. A deserted corridor. Which was exactly what she had said it would be. They came next to a cross corridor.

"Which way to the elevators?" Grayson whispered the question.

The woman pointed. And, after he had taken off his glasses, and stared at her fixedly—she quailed immediately—he repeated the question. She insisted in a quavering voice. So there seemed no doubt.

A minute later he opened another door, and there was the "basement" reception room. It was still too soon to feel relief, but there was a small, special excitement inside him as he guided her across the room toward the elevator section. Grayson did have to suppress a momentary impulse to open the door through which she had directed him that morning, and to which he had gone in the naïve belief that he would be interviewed by the Utt Commissioner. The impulse to look was momentary. The grim reality was that he didn't actually know what means had been used to stimulate the previously installed deep-trance hypnotism.

Take no unnecessary chances; that was his credo now. Out and up; that was his purpose.

All three elevators sat in a row at the bottom of their shafts. Enter the nearest. Press the "up" button. Wait, and experience a sense of relief, as the doors sedately slid shut. And wait again many minutes while the machine moved up, and up . . . and up.

There is a kind of death about anything interminable, thought Grayson. Like waiting for something to happen. And waiting. He tried to remember how long the down journey had seemed that morning. But that merely brought to mind a long-ago, wry observation that time past was not the same as time present. Besides, as he recalled it, he had tried to question his guide-guard. And, of course, conversation was a time devourer. . . . Maybe if I talk to Nora. No—consciously he rejected that solution. Not inside the elevator. It was apparent that she was not a co-conspirator; so that whatever additional information she might have could wait.

By his watch, the actual time of the up journey came to fifteen minutes and forty-three seconds. At that exact instant, the elevator stopped. It required a few more seconds for the door mechanism to function. But when it finally did—gulp!—it was the upper floor. The building floor. Quick, now, Nora! She must have felt as jittery as he, because it was quick. They half-ran across the lighted, deserted interior to the outside door. Would the latch release? Would the door open? It had *looked* that morning—despite his tension he had noticed it—like an ordinary tumbler-type lock, for which a key is required on the outside; but the knob does the unlocking from the inside.

The knob felt cool to his palm. It turned almost effortlessly. He pulled it open. A small breeze hit his face. He could see a sidewalk. And street lights. As he stood there, dazzled, Grayson had a thought.

. . . Is this an escape? Or is somebody deliberately letting us get away?—Somehow, it didn't matter to the exhilaration inside him. The future was a blur of threat. But that was something to be confronted in a minute or two.

Now was now. And it was perfect.

Chapter Nineteen

"Step down!" he said to the woman.

After she had done so, he stepped, himself. It was a small step in terms of distance. But, as he felt the hard pavement under his shoe, Grayson was aware of a warmth deep inside him. The feeling went deeper than exhilaration. It was a quietness, a sense of the rightness of things.

God! he thought. We surface-dwellers need to have access to the open spaces. We need to see the night sky, and to feel a wind blowing—

He had the woman by the arm again. Her feet seemed to drag as he guided her across the square. Something very deep in her, also, and so much of it that it was weakening her physically. The realization of what she must be going through made her briefly attractive again.

The bus that came along on their side of the street could have been the one he would have taken, had it occurred to him to check which one it was. He didn't look. He didn't care. Just get away, as a starter. The

Ipolsea motor of the bus must have been in perfect condition, because there was no sound as it glided away from the curb. The big machine moved swiftly along the bright street, wobbling now and then as the wheels sagged into little hollows in the concrete.

Grayson was doing his own looking, mostly to the rear to see if anyone was following. But of course they were soon away from the Utt Square. And so, as he faced forward again, he happened to glance at the woman. She was gazing avidly out through the windows. And what was contradictory about that was that her eyes were swollen with tears.

The physicist, who usually sat slumped and unobservant in buses, found himself trying to perceive what she was reacting to. As a consequence, in a real sense he saw the street scene for the first time in many a long year.

Even as he thought, What's going to happen to me? and What do I do now? and Will what I can do be effective? he was noticing the world of the city. And after a little he had an unexpected overall impression.

Peaceful. Most stores and places of business were closed at this hour of—he glanced automatically at his watch as he had the awareness—ten after nine.

Nevertheless, enough shops were open to stir the senses. Restaurants were open. And theaters, bowling alleys, exercise spas, computerized schools, religious centers, and cocktail bars—amazing! It was years since he had been in any places like that.

Momentarily, sobered by the recollection, he contemplated the darkness of his past years. Work all day, home all night, usually in his own room while Mila either remained in hers or sat in the living room, knitting.

The grim memory faded, and he thought wryly: Well, tonight is the night. And tomorrow. And maybe the next, also. For him, the time of the Total Threat had come. That seemed true. Logically, it seemed true.

First, by this time The Revolution would be looking for him.

And second, but not lesser, the Utt Maintenance group would be looking for him.

Surely, he had to act as if that were real, while he considered what he could, should, and would do.

Miss Patton and he climbed off the bus near the branch of an all-night bank with which the Haskett company dealt. They entered by way of the special night door with its lock control, a feature which—it occurred to Grayson for the first time—had been installed eight years ago.

Could the time be significant? Could *that* be when The Revolution had got under way in some kind of earnest?

—Something to check on later.

As he walked toward the night wicket, he noticed that Miss Patton seemed unalert and had a vague expression. It merely reminded him that she would be no help on this night of nights. Inwardly, he braced himself.

His problem: There was probably a hundred dollars in his billfold. His feeling: He needed more. Much more.

The check he presented was for four thousand dollars. It was Haskett Laboratory money, but he had departmental signature authority. His personal account required co-signing by Mila. The teller-computer hissed, huzzahed, and said: "Step out of line! Follow the arrows!"

Grayson sighed his disappointment. That fast, he thought resignedly. It meant—he was already identified. Well—a shrug—so be it!

The scene, as he stubbornly continued to stand there in the small lineup, had no appearance of threat. Four customers were behind him: two men and two women. Nora Patton was waiting off to one side, far enough away so that she had probably not heard the words spoken by the machine. The dull look was still on her face, so that was pretty certain.

A brightness caught Grayson's eyes, and he saw that they were made by the red arrows on the floor. His gaze followed the shiny little lines. They led to a closed door, behind which would obviously be a solid room. . . . Well, he thought again, more tolerantly, evidently they haven't had much time yet. So let's not delay.

He had already produced his duplicate of the first check. Now, he inserted it in the computer slot. Once more the buzz and the hiss. This time, as he anticipated, the money plopped into the receptacle.

Grayson said, "Thank you."

The machine said, "You're welcome."

In a manner of speaking, then, he sailed over to Miss Patton, and, grasping her arm, guided her rapidly toward the exit door. As that door automatically opened, he was thinking: —It really is valuable to know how things work!

Because it was used in every bank, the teller-computer was naturally a simple device. It, of course, only paid out money that was actually on deposit. And it could not be swindled. But it could be interfered with for any one person *one time*. The interruption completed, it cleared itself of barriers and was ready for the next transaction, or the next interrupting program.

They were outside again, and Grayson was feeling much better. He was also walking as quickly as he could move Miss Patton. At this stage, near a location where he had been challenged, he was a man in a hurry. Later, presumably, he could slow down and consider as a long-term problem the storm that he believed was building up for him.

Another bus. A brief ride to a dimly remembered cocktail lounge to which he had once taken an insistent woman buyer for lunch. The hostess jogged forward as Grayson and his escort entered (men were not allowed in bars without a woman companion). As the hostess tried to direct them, Grayson held back stubbornly, inquiring first where the phones were, and then asking to be seated near them.

The drinks ordered, he excused himself. Thereupon, he called his home, and at the same time watched the

Patton woman. That was to make sure she didn't slip away from him. It was unlikely, of course, because where would she go? But it was also grimly ironic. For all he knew, she was bugged. For all he knew, he would be traceable through her.

There was, of course, an even more personal possibility. *For all he knew,* he himself had been tampered with that very morning while he was unconscious. The morning really seemed long ago. Nevertheless, because of what had happened, he might be locatable no matter who he was with.

. . . The potential nightmare of either probability was only minutes, or hours, away. No matter. It would have to wait until he felt it safe to go to the laboratory.

Standing there at the phone counter, Grayson consciously resisted anxiety. Resisted in advance whatever, whoever, was about to threaten him.

By the time those thoughts completed, he had gone through his signal system on a home call. Two rings, then hang up. That disconnected the automatic answering service. Then he rang again.

On the second round, he could hear the phone at the other end ringing: one, two . . . five times. At that point finally came the click, the sound of a sigh, and then Mila's sad voice said, "Hello!"

Moments later she repeated the greeting, querulously. And Grayson realized that he had allowed the sadness in her voice to distract him. . . . What a basically intolerable thing she's doing, he decided wonderingly. All these years of instant rage, and now she wants sympathy— Still, since it was automatic, there could be no arguing with it, or discussing it, or reasoning about it. Accept or reject: those were his alternatives. And since he had already accepted, it was not a problem.

With that realization, he briskly identified himself, described an imaginary crisis in connection with the company—"several important buyers in town; I may not even get home"—and then asked the decisive question: "Any messages?"

There was one. "From Mr. Stan B-R-O-G-I-E—"
Mila spelled it out. She went on: "He said that if an
emergency developed in your deal tonight or tomorrow, to call him at—"

She paused for so long that Grayson gulped. And
had the fleeting consideration that somebody had cut
him off, or detoured his call with a view to making one
of those rapid number tracings.

Mila spoke again, more irritably: "It's hard to make
out Rosie's writing. You know how she is."

Grayson, abruptly grim, knew only too well. What
was teeth-gnashing about it was that, by answering at
all—when there was no signal for her to do so—she
interrupted the message-recording system, and thereby
prevented whoever was calling from doing the sensible
thing.

Rosie was a scrawler. Particularly was this true of
her memos for him, and she was absolutely vile with
numbers. Her fours looked like sevens. Her nines could
be fours. Threes and twos were often interchangeable.
And her figure for one actually looked like a three-
quarters-finished zero most of the time. What made
that deadly was that her zeros looked like curved ones.

A fleeting query did flick through Grayson's consciousness: —And where were you, my dear Mila, when
the phone rang, and Rosie answered? The call had to
have happened *since* he had emerged from the underground Utt prison. Which meant, within the last hour.

But he didn't say that aloud.

His hope had to be that his physical violence against
Rosie had chastened her. And evoked from her an attempt at legibility.

The number that Mila presently gave him had in it
a nine, a seven, a four, and a one. Accordingly, unless
the miracle had happened, it was almost certain to be
in error. And, of course, it would be impractical to try
all the likely variations, except through a computer.
So that, also, was for later.

Grayson thanked his wife, made a small, reassuring
personal remark, and returned to his seat in the booth,

with the distinct feeling of having been dealt a debilitating blow.

But he had one new possibility: At this critical hour, The Revolution was finally willing to be identified by the name of Steve Brogie.

Hard to believe, since Grayson had never heard the name before, that it could be anyone else calling his home. Not on this night when a man—himself—had deliberately abducted a woman employee from the inner sanctum of the Utt.

—We'll stay here for a while, he decided. Have a drink. Listen to the music. And see what materializes.

The music was supplied by a team of girl technicians who drew fantastic sounds out of a small but—Grayson knew—complicated electronic modulator. Although it was thirty years since he had danced, he insisted that the jittery Miss Patton join him on the flat space provided. Presently, he was guiding her stiff—but loosening—body over the glistening floor. And, simultaneously, keeping an eye on the entrance to the restaurant.

A ridiculous thing happened. Holding her in the dance position evoked physical attraction. Suddenly, his earlier caution was gone. In its place were mental images of Miss Patton as he had briefly seen her when she was naked. And there was also awareness that she had a slim body at the age of thirty-eight or forty, or whatever she was. And the thought that she was probably a suitable mistress for a man who had once dreamed of having six females at his disposition.

There was also an instant awareness of where he could take her for the night. Grayson Manufacturing maintained a permanent suite of rooms at a hotel a block or so from the company offices. It was for visiting buyers, and other similar types such as temporarily hired engineers who were wanted for specific jobs. . . . So far as Grayson could recall, not one of the four rooms in the suite was currently occupied.

—Won't even have to check in, he thought eagerly.

There was a short period of mental blankness after that return of lust. Then: —For God's sake, he told himself, doesn't a free man ever think of anything else . . . ? The shock was all the greater because the feeling had stolen in upon him so automatically, casually, at a time when he believed that great forces were moving out of the night against him. In fact—

His thought poised. For at that precise moment, a young woman in a traffic officer's uniform entered the restaurant. Grayson saw her pause. And watched as her eyes scanned, first, the tables, and then flicked toward the dancers—

. . . Fixed on him!

It was amazing with what confidence she immediately walked forward. Those years as a police officer, Grayson deduced, that daily round of telling people what to do, had reinforced the natural female ascendancy feelings she had acquired from growing up in a society were men were diminished by Utt law and Utt science. She clearly anticipated no problem.

But, in fact, Grayson hastily guided Miss Patton back to their table. And, as the traffic officer came up, he fired button four of his gas lapel-gun at the officer.

. . . Fatigue!

To feel it, or see it, is not necessarily to understand it. We look at what we call an exhausted person, and notice his haggard face and his listless, uncontrolled movements.

That is only the first stage of fatigue. In the second stage the individual becomes over-stimulated, appears tireless, and can, in fact, work all night with bright eyes and bright brain. Such a person does not look exhausted to us, or feel so to himself.

The fatigue parallel that Grayson's gas discharge induced in the young traffic officer was Stage Three. Nearly a century before, the physiologist Pavlov had performed the experiments that had resulted in the brainwash techniques of, first, Communist Russia, and then Communist China. . . . In this third stage of fatigue, the victim did a turnabout in his thought-feelings, and volunteered additional lies for the confession that had originally been suggested to him, all self-incriminating.

It was grim and deadly then. But it was interesting to biochemists, who later reasoned correctly that each stage was a chemical condition of the body. Therefore, it should be inducible by temporarily effective chemical injections.

It could.

The chemical for Stage Three was what Grayson discharged into the female traffic officer.

A tiny bit of suggestion at a key moment, and the recipient of the chemical compound suddenly knew what he was supposed to change to—without, of course, noticing the process.

The young woman traffic officer, at Grayson's suggestion to "join me and become a part of my work force," obligingly sat down at the table, and reported that she was "ready to do her duty."

"Which is what?" asked Grayson, taking no chances.

"Whatever you command."

"Very good," he replied. "Right now, I think you'd better guide this lady and myself safely out of here."

It was interesting to him, then, that she commandeered their passage through the restaurant kitchen and out of a side door. Outside, she cautiously led the way along a back alley to a side street where several unoccupied traffic control cars were parked. She unlocked the door of one of these, and said, "Quick, get in!"

Patton and Grayson climbed onto the rear seat, and the young woman in uniform slipped behind the wheel, and started the silent Ipolsea motor. Moments later, the machine glided away from the curb; and then at his request she gave him the history of how she had come to the restaurant.

Her name was Doris Lesser.

Her "confession": "I am a lieutenant in the traffic control department. My hours are from six P.M. until midnight. I was driving my usual route twenty-one minutes ago when I received an A-zero call on my

Two-Way. A-zero, that's urgent. Top priority. I have not previously in my three years and eight months as a control driver had a top-priority call.

"A picture of you, Dr. Grayson, was then shown on the car screen. I was told that the location lines crossed at the Yellow Barn Restaurant. When I arrived at the restaurant, I checked to see what other control cars had already shown up, or were in process. As you saw, there were three on this side. There are three more up front, and several others on the way. We girls drew lots as to who would go in, and I won——"

Grayson asked quickly, "No mention of Miss Patton here?"

"None."

The man leaned back relieved. . . . So it's all me——

Silently, he criticized his intelligence at the moment of coming to in the "box" room that morning. . . . I probably scratched the skin where they fired the locator device into me—tiny, tiny little thing, only a few molecules in diameter, but undoubtedly it put forth a detectable impulse. Small though it was, it was large enough to have caused a skin irritation during those first minutes after he awakened. Such devices drew their energy from the host body.

He sat, now, eyes closed, striving to remember where it was he had itched. Obviously, he must have reached up in the time-honored way, and cozily rubbed at the irritated area with his fingernails. No memory came.

It was not a decisive barrier to action. With a frown, he reached into a pocket. Found the carefully torn hole with its patch. Removed the patch. And, inserting two fingers, drew out the hysteresis device.

In the three-quarter darkness of the back seat (lighted only by the street lights they passed), he could, first, feel the thin, soft fabric, with its in-woven metal wires, its tiny circuits, and its heat battery. And then he was able to see the little gleaming wires that were the visible part of the circuit design.

To activate the first stage, all he need do was place his hand over the battery, hold it there until the warmth energized the plates. And then slide the fabric device over likely locations of his body.

It required moments only to do the energizing. Whereupon, he made a tentative slide over his left forearm, then over the right forearm. Nothing happened. There was no swift, intense burning sensation inside the arm.

Grayson hesitated. His problem was that he did not really want to be unlocatable. Not permanently. And, of course, there was no way to make it a temporary condition. So—

With a sigh, he slipped the hysteresis device back into his pocket, and thought: All right, all right, I'll wait. And decide later. Right now, let's see what else they bring up against me.

The decision made, his next moves followed automatically—it seemed to him. He instructed Officer Lesser to pull over to the curb near a bus stop. When she had done so, he gave her three hundred dollars and a key to the hotel suite.

After he had named the hotel, and its location, and what bus to take to get there, he said, "In the morning go out and buy a woman's wig and a long-sleeved dress that will fit over my head and my clothes. Right now, take a size-estimating look at me—"

He finished: "If I'm still uncaptured, I'll park near the hotel entrance at—" He paused to consider how much time it would take her to get the wig and the dress, allowing for most stores not opening before ten o'clock. "—at eleven-fifteen A.M. Get there as soon as you can after that."

The younger woman promised faithfully; and he thereupon had Miss Patton climb out first. After which he whispered to Miss Lesser, "Don't let her get away. Keep her with you, if necessary."

She nodded. Then: "You will, of course, be coming to see me during the night."

Grayson actually said, "Uh!" But he was able, then, to restrain a further awkward response. What he was belatedly remembering was that the Stage Three fatigue conversion evoked a special affectionate reaction from its victim for the victimizer. And the person treated by the chemical that accomplished the same purpose usually felt that affection for his (her) tormentor.

Grayson found his voice. "Not tonight," he said, "but soon—" He broke off. "Quick, here comes the bus. On your way."

A minute or so later, as the bus was driving off, and there he was alone with the police car, he had the startled realization that he had not driven an automobile since he was sixteen.

Chapter Twenty

Grayson climbed gingerly into the driver's seat of the patrol car. Closed the door. And sat there.

All around him was the bright night of downtown. It was a familiar city scene for him. He had lived in the place since leaving college nearly thirty years earlier.

He was, the realized, not in a hurry. And that was an oddly good feeling. . . . "In a way, I'm on top of this situation—"

He spoke the words aloud. After a moment, after he had been silent a little—and there was only the echo of them in his head—they sounded ridiculous.

Yet the feeling did not entirely go away. . . .

Just to make sure that he would be able to leave if he wished, Grayson placed his left foot on the brake, released the emergency, and stepped lightly on the accelerator with his right foot.

There was an immediate feedback of small vibration through his shoes and up his legs. The car tugged—a little.

It was an unmistakable signal. He could go forward.

That was the beauty of the Ipolsea motor. It was always "on." Like the sun and the moon and the planets from which the Ipolsea core derived, not its power but its stimulus.

The awareness of motor vibration energy stirred Grayson unexpectedly. He eased his foot off the brake. And turned the steering wheel. Like a glider released from its attachment, the car swung out from the curb. And, since he had taken the precaution to look to the rear, and make sure no one was coming, there he was, learning to drive again.

During the first hour that was it. He was like a man who had, long ago, played the piano. So, now, he was finally sitting once more at the keyboard familiarizing his fingers and his nervous system with and to all those complex movements. Except, remembering how, between ages thirteen and sixteen, he had driven cars on his father's farm, this was much easier.

There were some bad moments. Drivers kept turning in from side streets and following him closely. The bad moments were when he swung onto other streets—and they swung with him. Three times it seemed as if he had no choice but to park and confront. Before he was ready. Before he had thought it through.

Each time, when he did draw up at a curb, and braced himself for battle, the "pursuing" machine, with its female driver, casually glided past, and on, and away.

Actually, it fitted. The truth—Grayson told himself —is that there's only a tiny group of Utt-authorized human schemers. In the pits: a man's and a woman's voice gave the orders.

The fact was, the Utt had created a human civilization that just about ran itself. But it did need a small maintenance crew. By now the members of that crew would be curious about him.

All right, he thought decisively, I can drive. I'm ready. . . . As ready as he could hope to be, in view of the fact that he was driving a police patrol car.

He pulled over to a curb where it was dark, and parked. Then he stretched out on the front seat. It did not, it seemed to Grayson, matter if he slept or not. The passage of time was the important thing.

He must have slept at once. Because his next awareness was of opening his eyes. And of staring up into the barrel of a gun held by a man who had somehow gotten silently into the rear seat. A man who said, "Well, so we got you, eh? And within twenty-four hours."

Grayson didn't move. Not a decision, that. Simply, the voice spoke its triumph. And in all those first seconds, Grayson, in spite of his expectation that something like this would happen, reacted with an automatic emotion that was probably fear.

What happened next—the gun drew back. The man who held it settled into the rear seat, and continued to point the weapon, at a distance now. "You better take a minute to wake up," he said.

For a second, or two, or three, after those words were spoken, Grayson thought of them as indicators, of all things, of goodwill.

That feeling of almost reassurance came to an abrupt end, as the man added curtly, "Right now what we want from you is some wide-awake answers. And they'd better be good."

The first thing Grayson noticed, after that threat was uttered, was that he had come to, and was, in fact, surprisingly wide awake. Which brought the relieving realization that he must have slept quite a few hours. It was relieving because it meant that he was ready for the long day ahead.

Ouside the car it was still dark. And yet he realized that if he had been asked, at the moment of coming to, his first impression of his assailant's appearance, he would have described him as dark-haired, with a square

face, about forty years old. A mature age. . . . Since it
was bright enough now for that much visual perception,
night must indeed be yielding to an early version of
dawn.

There was another, somewhat less satisfying, awareness in Grayson's mind. Unfortunately, this dark-haired
man was probably not a top leader. Gaining control of
him would therefore not be significant. And inadvisable
except in self-defense.

As Grayson sort of settled into his twisted position,
half-turned toward the rear seat, and with his new
awarenesses crowding in on him, the dark-haired one
said earnestly, "You must realize that I could have shot
you as you slept, after I first arrived. Do you realize
that?" The final words were pointedly spoken, as if
a reply was mandatory.

Grayson said in an even tone that, yes, he realized.

Yet even as he spoke the words, he had the startled
thought that the threat of death had, somehow, not
seemed immediate. At once, he realized what the factor
was. Incredibly, in a remote part of his mind was a
belief that the Utt were not basically evil, and not
killers insofar as the general populous was concerned.
In fact, he had thought of them as do-gooders who
had misread human nature, and misjudged particularly
the human male. That was a while back. He wasn't
so sure anymore about the misjudgment.

It was hardly the kind of explanation to give at this
moment. And, besides, there was another purpose, more
acceptable—it seemed to him.

He spoke it in the same quiet tone. Explained that he
had hoped the power group would want to find out how
he had escaped from their underground prison. Find it
out, that is, before they did anything against him.

In front of him, the square face changed. Twisted
into a frown. "Just a minute," said the man in an astonished tone, "you mean, you *expected* somebody like
me would show up the way I did?"

"I hoped," replied Grayson, in the same steady voice,

"that the higher-ups of the Utt-authorized maintenance people would be contactable. And, naturally, the chances of my finding them were much dimmer than of their finding me."

"Oh!" The other man nodded, half to himself. "It was a chance you decided to take. But why? What do you gain?"

"What I'm interested in at this stage," said Grayson, truthfully, "is to find out where you people really stand. Do you get real personal power and affluence from an Utt-controlled world? Or are you hoping that someday we can, uh, persuade them to leave?"

Slowly, the man leaned back in his seat. He seemed to be coming to a decision. Abruptly, he spoke: "Ted, what do you think?"

The question was so obviously addressed to someone else that Grayson correctly deduced that his assailant had a communication line open to a back-up attack group. Even as he had the thought, a voice spoke from a concealed electronic device high up on the other man's coat.

The voice said cryptically, "Dr. Grayson is now established to be a man with whom we shall have to deal in some thorough fashion, Dick."

Ted. And Dick. Grayson took note of the names.

He also noticed the implication of threat in Ted's words. But he decided not to be discouraged. Fundamentally, these maintenance people were as controlled as the rest of humankind. And they needed help as much as anyone. His hope had to be that they realized it.

So he said, quietly, "I'm sure we can work out the details on how thorough."

Dick seemed not to hear. Seemed, in fact, to be listening intently to something that Grayson couldn't hear. An ear speaker?—the scientist wondered. If so, the communication here was going on at two levels, only one of which the victim was being allowed to listen to.

The second level of communication was abruptly deducible as having been a question. For Dick said, "So far I have no impression that he has done anything to take control of me. So he must be intending to reason with us."

Since, presumably, that remark was intended for him also, Grayson interjected, "Any reasoning I'm doing is not directed at you, Ted, or you, Dick. It is intended for your superiors. What are the chances of their being advised of this conversation?"

"They're listening in," said Ted's voice, cheerfully. "So the chances are pretty good, I'd guess. The big point we want explained are those remarks you made to Herb Lartmore at the gate of Hell. You seemed to imply in what you said that you understood how that intense heat was generated down there?"

It was Grayson's turn for a long pause. And for a sudden shaky feeling.

But there was also an intermediate reaction. Herb Lartmore? Somehow, it had not occurred to him that Herb was one of the power group.

Ted's voice was continuing: "We've had some very good scientists in our group try to figure out what that is down there. And they have no idea. Do you?"

"Yes," said Grayson.

"Are you going to tell us?" Ted's voice asked.

"No," replied Grayson.

He had a mental picture, sitting there, of a long line of the top leadership of the Utt-authorized maintenance people hearing that refusal. Impossible, of course, for him to know what their reaction was. But he could deduce that they had many times committed murder in the past, and that they must believe they could force the information from him.

Grayson hoped they couldn't. The colossal, deadly reality down there would, if it were revealed, terrify everyone. He believed sincerely that in everyone's mind —except his own—all thought of resistance to the Utt would cease. No change in the Utt-created system would be allowed. Forever.

Ted's voice was speaking again: "Can you control what's down there?"

The answer was no. But, naturally, he couldn't admit that. Grayson said, "It's going to require some thinking and experimenting."

"But in the long run—maybe?"

"Absolutely," Grayson lied.

He became aware that the man—Dick—was stirring. He leaned slightly forward. From that position he said, "Sir, I have just been instructed to tell you that most of us upper-echelon maintenance people have long been waiting for somebody with the brain and the training— and the proof that he could act. And when, so to say, we watched you—without knowing how you did it— break out of hell . . ." He shrugged. "It seemed as if we finally had our leader, sir, against the Utt."

His jaw tightened. His dark eyes narrowed. "Dr. Grayson, we've got to kick those S.O.B. Utt off this planet, and get men back into control. What do you say? Will you talk to us?"

The incredible! First, The Revolution wanted him as leader. Now, the Human Establishment! The people whom he had taken for granted had privileges and power under the Utt.

Grayson drew several deep breaths. Because he couldn't help thinking of the portion of a blue sun that was down there. And couldn't help thinking that these people must never be allowed to realize that if that sun ever was triggered into pouring its energy outward, outward, a planet the size of earth would dissolve in a single haze of flame.

They would knuckle under. That was his conviction. He wouldn't. At least, not until he had studied all the evidence. That was the scientific way. And, also—he had a feeling deep, deep in his being—it was the way of something indomitable in the human male.

It was that "chin-up" feeling which now utilized his

voice box, and said, "Why don't you begin by giving me some data? We can go on from there."

Grayson drew a deep breath. Sitting there in the brightening morning, he actually had the deluded feeling that he was ready.

Chapter Twenty-one

It was a council, not of war, but of practicality.

How long since anyone had seen an Utt? That was the question that could finally be asked of key people. The answer: Apparently, seventeen years ago a grief-stricken wife had waylaid an Utt outside the Utt building. The super-being, thus accosted, wafted himself into the air above her. And then went back into the Utt building.

After letting the time involved sink in to the dozen and a half persons assembled in the laboratory conference room, Grayson said softly, "I think we must act as if the Utt have long ago departed, leaving their control systems to be managed by human beings. And why don't we leave those systems in operation, except that we change the rules slightly in a way that takes proper account of human nature?"

He finished: "That way the outward appearance will be the same, in the event that another Utt ship comes to take a look."

No one argued. It was as if they all believed in the

same omnipotent deity. And they had no intention of ever offending *that*. Yet each group wanted to collaborate with the others within the frame of the omnipower; yet simultaneously create a system that fitted the realities.

What were those realities? No one argued about that, either.

With, in effect, a god looking over everybody's shoulder, they agreed that only genuine criminals (the essentially violent people) should be kept down in the pits. A healthy woman who failed to give sex to her husband on an average of once a week could be replaced by a woman who would. Likewise, impotent males were discardable. Men who were willing to wear women's clothing, and look shaven while they did so, could drive cars under those conditions.

It was agreed that special precautions should be devised to safeguard the repair tape that rendered spectacles harmless. And, in exchange for modifying the formula and taking the present version off the market, the Haskett Laboratories would have additional business diverted to it.

Finally, because of his unusual scientific understanding, and his numerous affirmative actions of the past little while, in all the world he would be the ultimate male authority.

There was one development in the days and weeks that followed that disturbed Grayson.

He had taken it for granted that he would resume a stable homelife with Mila. It didn't work that way.

Miss Haskett, who had sat silent and unobtrusive in the back of the conference room during that first meeting, came into his office later. As she stated her point of view: "The use of my property for such meetings requires that you and I operate on a level of trust such as normally exists between a husband and wife."

Incredibly, it had not occurred to Grayson that a rebel group using someone's property for a meeting place thereby compromised that property. As the reality hit him, he said, "Yes, uh!"

It was late afternoon the next day when he found Miss Lesser waiting outside for him in her police car. He got in quickly, at her gesture. As she drove, she pointed out to him that, in associating with him, she had, in effect, become his spy inside the police department; and from that there was now no escape for her or for him.

"Uh!" said a startled Grayson. "Yes, uh!"

But the most unexpected development was a phone call from, and a subsequent rendezvous with, Nora Patton. She reported a miracle. Henceforth, she would be allowed a half-day visit to the surface once a week. She didn't exactly word her proposition like blackmail. But somehow she conveyed the reality that, as the person who knew how he had got to the surface, and as the person who would in future be a quiet observer for him of the underground world, it was important that they meet each time she came to the surface with her week's information.

"Uh!" said Grayson. "Uh, yes."

He was the man who hoarded within himself the awful secret of the blue sun. On occasion at night he woke up from a hideous dream of that utter hell of heat, seething ceaselessly in a hundred locations under the surface of the planet.

No question, he needed a spy system.

And it really wasn't all that bad.

As the days glittered by, and each woman kept him to his unwritten contract, he was occasionally amazed at his capacity. . . . Perhaps, he analyzed, it was the fact that he had been forced into these relationships; and therefore he didn't have to feel guilty. Perhaps, it was simply a sex-starved male making up for thirty-five years of nothing. Whatever, his body came through nobly.

Every monthly meeting of the council had more people showing up: key establishment personnel from other parts of the country, and, after a little, from other parts of the world. Some of them listened silently to the discussion. Others participated. In the end, all without exception came over and shook Grayson's hand. Many of them went off with ears in their eyes.

It had been a long purgatory, with no hope in sight —until, suddenly, this!

Another day. The special intercom from the owner's office buzzed. Grayson pressed the button. "Yes, Miss Haskett?" It was the formal response between them for the benefit of any outer office staff, who might be passing either his open door or hers. .

Surprisingly, there was a pause. A long pause. And then—her stricken voice came: "Mr. Grayson, an Utt has just walked into my office. It's here to see you."

In his time, Grayson had had the chilling experience of stepping off a curb just as a car whipped around the corner. The thrill of leaping back spasmodically, and barely making it—this was like that. And once he had been striding, and he had topped a rise, and found himself swaying back with one leg poised above the edge of an abyss.

At such moments the body produced electrical currents of astonishing, unpleasant intensity. Something to do with an unbalance between the two nervous systems. An instant, awful feeling. Monetary blankness.

All that was in the pause, and the silence with which his total being responded to the terrible message. Finally, a sembiance of reason. "Send him in!" Grayson croaked.

Chapter Twenty-two

At one minute after one, Mila came out of the house, and took up a waiting stance at the curb. Two and a quarter minutes later, a car with a young woman in it—the driver—pulled over to the curb, and stopped. Mila climbed into the front seat with the driver. Whereupon, the machine silently glided off down the street, heading away from the center of the city. Miss Lesser made a U-turn, and followed.

Grayson did not argue with himself as to why he was here. . . . He had scooted from his office by way of his personal exit, because, when your basic theory —that there were no Utt remaining on earth—was suddenly proved wrong . . . the early childhood impulse, not exactly to go home to mother but something like that, took over.

Once outside, he used his private channel to Miss Lesser; that was no problem. And, since she kept a supply of women's clothing in the trunk of her car just for him, that also answered his desperate need.

And here he was. Mentally almost blank. Yet something had surfaced. His first, vague plan had been, simply, to take evasive action while he—as he put it to himself—evaluated the situation. Despite the vagueness, within minutes the thought about Mila came out of wherever it had been lurking. He even, in a faraway fashion, argued silently that pursuit of the mystery of Mila's daytime whereabouts was important for him to do. Better than just running. It was a decision to act.

As more minutes went by, and as the car ahead moved purposefully through the traffic, amazement came anew. How . . . amazing . . . that all these amicable weeks Mila had not volunteered a word of explanation.

Where they went, all four of them—Mila and her driver in one car, and Grayson, striving to be determined again, and Miss Lesser in the other—was to a large shopping complex at the south end of the city. The central building of the cluster was a high-rise structure of thirty-five stories. There was an auto entrance with the sign: FOR RESIDENTS AND VISITORS TO HEAVEN ONLY. The car with Mila turned onto the ramp. They did it so abruptly that Miss Lesser seemed confused. But she put on the brake. And that made it possible, after a long hesitation, for her to turn carefully, and slowly, into what turned out to be an ascending spiral driveway.

"Keep following!" said Grayson.

What happened presently was one of those minor nuisances. Close though they were to Mila's car, somehow another machine from another floor edged between them. So there they were, first one car behind, then two, then three. And, finally, it was a matter of trusting that Mila's driver had not turned aside, and was still going on and up, somewhere ahead.

Grayson was leaning back, tense, in his seat. He was dimly conscious that he was somewhat more aware of his surroundings. Losing contact with Mila's car had actually produced an alerting emotion: exasperation. That first intruding vehicle—Miss Lesser had hesitated as it nosed in. The appearance was of courtesy. His disappointed feeling was that it wouldn't have happened if he had been driving. And, of course, that was a totally useless thought. To be forever relegated to that portion of the universe in which were gathered all the might-have-beens of human and individual history.

Up and up they went. He had time to have a thought about himself and his fate: . . . If the Utt know what I've been doing the last few months, then I'm in trouble—

Consciously, he braced himself against the fear that came. It was a conscious bracing because he was now the leader of the Utt opposition. Leaders—it was a stereotype—must not flinch.

Some time after that, farther and higher up that incredible ramp, he was still tensing his body in protest and resistance when . . . a sound from Miss Lesser. She gestured. And there at last was what Grayson, without thinking about it, had been waiting for. It was a sign with the words: 34TH FLOOR. PARKING AREA. An arrow pointed.

A line of other arrows guided all the cars. Everywhere, now, that Grayson looked, women were driving into tiny stalls, getting out, and walking off in the same general direction. Miss Lesser drove uncertainly into one of the stalls. She turned and explained her uncertainty: "I'm hoping these places aren't reserved."

That was surely the least of Grayson's problems. Who would be concerned, he didn't know. But if someone later found an unmarked police car in one of the parking spaces, it could not easily affect him.

He made an effort, then, to visualize what was happening from the viewpoint of an onlooker. As he saw it, Miss Lesser and he had the outward appearance of being two women geting out of an automobile. All around them other women were doing the same. . . . Two unobserved (Grayson told himself) females who, after a tiny hesitation while they determined exactly where the others were going, joined the crowd. After that they were part of what seemed to be an unending straggle of womankind.

It was interesting to Grayson that about half the females were in their early twenties, and the other half were middle-aged. Could the older ones all be guides? And the younger, new initiates?

It made a kind of sense in view of the minuscule information he had got from Rosie. Initiates to what? Today, perhaps, he would find out what the Utt had been secretly requiring all these years from the females of the human species.

There were other tall women . . . Grayson was presently relieved to notice. And even some who were sturdy in the shoulders. His disguise seemed secure.

The strung-out lines of women led the way to a perfectly mundane row of escalators, all going up. Grayson stood on the step below Miss Lesser, waiting for what the thirty-fifth floor might bring, and thinking, baffled: So this is where Mila may have been coming all these years!

Amazing that even now no memory came of what Rosie had fearfully blabbed out to him. A place called Heaven—and there was not the faintest stirring in him of having heard Rosie say such an unusual word.

Moments after that frustrated realization, he had his first view of the thirty-fifth floor.

Chapter Twenty-three

A wide area, like an office building lobby (but without elevators), was what he saw first. Then, a puzzle: a series of shelves—that aligned with each escalator—with, of all things, pairs of overshoes on them. Piles and piles, and rows and rows, of them.

As he saw the display, Grayson hesitated. At which moment, a woman's voice spoke from a hidden speaker. She said, "Walk straight ahead! Select a pair of overshoes that fit your feet, and put them on! Then proceed into the corridor directly in front of you!"

That, Grayson perceived, was exactly what the women were doing. Each individual female, as she came off the escalator, did go through the shelving directly in front of her. And did put on a pair of overshoes.

And walked on into a glossy corridor, as instructed.

When Grayson, obeying those same orders, came to the overshoes, he saw that they were arranged according to size. The largest were on the top shelf, the smallest on the bottom. For him, it took extra time while he fumbled awkwardly over several pairs on the top shelf. He had, of course, to make a quick estimate of size. It worked. Principally, it worked because the overshoes were the stretch kind. His feet slipped cozily into them. As he continued on into the corridor extension, with its flat, gleaming walls, he told himself that "cozily" was the best way to describe a tight fit.

It was interesting, also, to a person like himself, who noticed small details, that the unseen woman's voice repeated its message twice more while he was within hearing. (So there must be other new people here today who didn't know the rules.)

As he walked on, keeping his place in line behind Miss Lesser, he was pleased to notice that he was beginning to be tolerant of himself and of where he was. . . . I am doing something that I should have done long ago. If I ever do talk to an Utt, I should know the whole score, not just a part of it—

As he continued, then, walking, Grayson saw that some distance ahead the line of women was making another turn. Because it was a distance, he had time, unfortunately, to feel guilty again. During the past few months, somehow, he had managed to fight off that feeling of wrongness. Incredibly, like the men of pre-Utt days, he had accepted all too easily that there was no way that he could refuse the women. And that in fact a "leader" had to pay whatever price was necessary for, for example, having Miss Lesser and her police car available today.

He was, moments later, still arguing weakly against that brand of logic . . . when his part of the line reached the turn. It proved to be a right-angled turned into, this time, a narrow hallway, barely wide enough for one person at a time.

The feeling that something was now going to happen penetrated the outer surface of his mental turmoil. Automatically, he reached out and grabbed Miss Lesser's shoulder. His fingers held her back, as he stepped in front of her.

And found himself walking a scant three feet behind

a woman who needed to lose weight. Her blonde hair didn't seem to fit the rest of her; so he presumed it was artificial. There were four women ahead of her. In the fleet of seconds during which his perception encompassed the five females, somehow he missed what happened to Number One, ten feet ahead.

But Number Two turned left—and stepped out of sight. And so did Three, Four, and Artificial Blonde. Except that, when A.B. did it, he was close enough, so that he saw that she was alone in a little alcove. And he saw her left arm and hand move as if to push at something. And Grayson was thinking, they all seem to know what to do. (Or at least seemed to accept that they would follow the person ahead; certainly, no voice was directing them now.) . . . And he was thinking: How long has this been going on . . . ? And he was thinking: Will there be an Utt present where we're going . . . ? And he was thinking: Maybe I should go back to my office, and to hell with it—

The train of thoughts ceased with an inner crash of confusion.

Because A.B. was gone. What, what, what!

Grayson had paused, one foot raised for his next step forward. Slowly, he lowered it until he was standing, almost bracing himself against the floor. But already he was rationalizing what he had seen. Mostly, he felt self-criticism. Damn fool! He should have been watching her with total absorption. Instead—his attention was on a bunch of inner nothingness. Artificial Blonde must have simply gone through the door.

It looked—now that his attention was focusing—like a gray-blue door panel. Very flat surface. The appearance was of metal. And the only baffling thing was that he could see no lines. Nothing visible to show where the door was set into the wall. Okay . . . he thought wearily—I'll push at it the way she did. And go through without knowing where or what.

He raised his arm. Extended his fingers. He intended to push very slowly at the flat surface in front. As far as he could recall afterward, no part of his hand actually, then, touched anything.

Something grabbed his palm all the way back to the wrist. And pulled. He staggered forward, drawn by that tugging jerk at his hand. He shuddered from head to toe. Vision blanked. Sound receded. And then—

He was in a huge arena. And the floor was a good ten feet below him. And—

He was "floating."

Chapter Twenty-four

From that very first moment, being scientifically trained, Grayson did his trying-to-understand-with-his-knowledge.

He noticed that it was not only he who was in the air. All around him, female bodies were suspended between the floor and a high ceiling. They "floated" as he was doing. For a mind, educated as his was, the whole thing was utterly impossible.

He had been mentally braced to do something. To have some purpose on his arrival beyond the door. And he actually flailed the air, in his total surprise. But even then the second act of noticing was already occurring: A new awareness of the size of the room. The ceiling was an astounding hundred feet above the floor. And an amazing distance away—more than a hundred yards—was the nearest wall. And the way that was, was the most meaningless of all. It was made of a glossy black substance which had stars painted on it.

That was, in that first look, a brief noticing only.

It included the awareness that the glossy wall seemed to be circular, and extended all the way around him. Although he did not look behind him to verify.

His third noticing was actually his attention returning to what he had, really, never stopped noticing: the number of women who were sharing his fantastic experience. Simply, in an area that extended all those distances that he had observed, from a few feet above the floor to a few feet below the ceiling, were female bodies.

At least—Grayson now had his first modifying thought—they were all dressed like women. Obviously, there could be a few bold, sly males dressed in women's clothing spying on this situation, as he was doing. Oddly, he didn't really believe that; it was just a thought of a grown man who could have complex considerations. Even as he had that thought, he was estimating that there were probably a thousand women suspended in the great air space around him.

And still he did not look around. Did not even glance back to see if Miss Lesser had been catapulted somewhere behind him. He floated. And waited, with the appearance of accepting his situation. That was exactly what the women were doing; and so, in a way, his purpose was to make no move that might attract attention.

Moments later he was floating there, apparently just one more anonymous unit of a vast throng—when he grew aware that the back of his right hand was tingling.

Grayson froze. Then, carefully, holding the hand so that the tingling continued, he looked at it. Observed the exact way the hand slanted. The directional he got was toward the ceiling, off to one side.

He pressed his left-hand middle finger hard into the center of that palm. Which at once synchronized the tingling direction finder with a laser gun embedded in the shoulder padding of his suit. He heard an ever so faint hissing sound as the invisible beam fired slantingly up at the spy ray mechanism, or whatever it was, that had spotted him.

What was relieving, instantly, was that the tingling stopped.

But now he was resigned. He had reacted as fast as was possible against a threat that required a conscious human decision. Yet the delay between the first signal and the reaction, in electronic terms, was considerable. In the interval, an alarm could have sounded. And a living somebody could have noticed.

Stronger than before came the feeling: now you have to do something basic. It occurred to him, as he continued to contemplate the unfortunate development, that a spy ray system in the ceiling implied that there was, in fact, a thirty-sixth floor. Or, at least, an attic inside which a human being could crawl.

That seemed to be a contradiction. The signs on the way into the building, and as they climbed, had stated that this was a thirty-five story structure. So what was up there was a mystery which—so the automatic feeling of purpose required of him—he would now have to solve.

But, first, I'll have to get to the floor. Second, I'll have to remain inconspicuous. And, third—

That was vaguer. That was back to the primary puzzlement about the impossible thing that had happened. All of these women, and himself, up here in the air.

That thought ended suddenly. Because he had started to look around again. And in doing so saw that some women were already down on the floor. And others were in process of *going down*.

As he watched these latter, he had his first clue. The method was absolutely sensational to a scientist like himself.

Near Grayson, a women shoved upward at the feet of another woman who was accidentally above her. The shover was precipitated to the floor. The shoved went up to the ceiling. Arrived there, she deliberately pushed at it. And down *she* went to the floor, also.

Hey! thought an astounded Grayson. *That's the third law of motion.*

Instant corollary: But there is no force being applied

to hold me up. That must mean—it was an immediate concomitant—there's no gravity.

But—

All around him, as his mind poised before an awesome array of contradictions, other women were pushing at each other. Action and reaction. Some of them used their skirts to trap the air, and shove at it like a bird's wing, flapping.

Whatever the method, down to the floor they went. And, at the moment of landing, placed their feet flat on the floor. And then—

Each woman walked as if at each step she had to pull that foot out of quicksand. Or—Grayson recognized abruptly—as if the sole was magnetically attaching . . . at each step . . . to an iron or steel floor.

So that's why we've got those overshoes. They have magnetized soles.

Abruptly, the clues were *enough*.

Figuratively, his gaze flew again to the glossy black walls, with the pictures on them of the starry heavens. The great thought that came—a dazzling revelation—was: Those are not pictures of stars. They *are* stars in black space as seen through a transparent plastic.

A window! We're in an orbiting spacecraft.

Somehow, as they walked from the parking lot on Floor 34 up to Floor 35, and into that tiny alcove, a thousand women and he had crossed a barrier. Unnoticing, feeling nothing, no sense of movement through space, no momentary blackout at the instant of transition from the building to . . . twenty-four thousand miles up. Maybe farther.

Even as he kept adjusting his mind, even as the event grew and grew inside him, as he tried to evaluate the incredibly advanced physics required, another, more human, feeling began to move along a parallel track on the feeling level of his being. A sinking sensation. An awareness of the impossibility of anyone on earth —any human—resisting the super-race that could achieve this marvel of mass transportation.

But at least—he thought—now I know how to get down to the floor.

Feeling more resigned than anything else, he was about to do exactly that—go "down"—when . . .

The tingling began once more on the back of his hand.

Chapter Twenty-five

Fear!

Grayson felt the blood drain from his cheeks. And it was that, presently, that he noticed. And it braced him slightly. Because—I'll be damned . . . it was a physiologic reaction, not dependent on gravity. It seemed to mean that bloodflow inside his body related to the physics of liquids moving through pipes under pressure.

He was balancing himself by this time. And taking directional readings—as before. Unfortunately, this time, when he fired his invisible beam . . . the tingling continued.

Okay, okay—resigned. Superior science has taken over. As if something analyzed the problem. And solved it.

So—first—get to the floor. Then decide what to do about the detector system that was now permanently zeroed in on him.

Permanently, meaning as long as he was in the

vicinity. And he wasn't leaving yet. Because, there actually was no place for him to go.

It was really time. During those minutes of his strange battle with an electronic spy system, eighty percent of the women had precipitated themselves in what he still thought of as the . . . downward . . . direction. And those that remained were rapidly descending to join them.

Within minutes, anyone remaining in the air would look conspicuous.

Hastily, with that thought, Grayson now, finally, made another, larger survey of that giant room. All the way around. And there, indeed, behind him—about forty feet—was Miss Lesser. The moment he turned, she waved frantically. Too wildly. The action tipped her over on her back. In a manner of speaking, then, she lay there, struggling a little, but obviously with no clear idea of how she had tilted herself, or of what to do about it.

Grayson used his dress, as some of the women had done, like a bird's wing to flail his lean body over to her. He grasped her arm as he floated by. And at her ear he spoke the necessary instruction about what to do when she reached the floor.

(What he meant by floor was not a point that he tried to explain to her.)

He did as the others had done: shoved gently. She went "down." He went "up." There, like so many women—the guides, he presumed—had done before him, he placed his hands on what turned out to be a smooth surface. And shoved himself back the way he had come.

He managed by dint of maneuvering to land on a bare space. Thereupon, he did what he had instructed Miss Lesser to do: placed both feet squarely on that surface. As it had for a thousand women, the method worked for him perfectly. His magnetized overshoes grabbed, and held. And thereby the surface became a floor for him, also.

That "floor" had already revealed a second quality.

Everywhere women—again, it had to be the guides who
would know—were bending down. Inserting fingers into
slots. And pulling out and up . . . a chair that remained
attached by its back legs, unfolded, and became a seat.

Grayson took note of which direction the chairs
faced. Which meant he located the stage, also. Calmly,
but firmly, and somewhat awkwardly—the magnetized
soles kept clinging at each step—he led Miss Lesser
toward the rear of what, in the space of a few minutes,
had become a large auditorium. They ended up sitting
in the back row.

The physicist sat there kind of blank, it seemed to
him.

And so he did not immediately notice the scientific
superiority feeling he was experiencing. . . . Can it be
that this is why the Utt refused all women of earth
the privilege of becoming scientists? So that they would
be vulnerable to the belief that this *is* heaven . . . ? The
phenomenon, to untrained minds, must be absolutely
awesome.

Suddenly, he visualized Mila as she had been all
these years. Somebody would, of course, have "guided"
her up here. Her subsequent actions, examined in
retrospect, showed total acceptance at the overwhelm
level. And, until recently—until *he* changed—her only
escape had been an occasional drunken bout. Of which
she had no memory afterward.

The superiority attitude continued. But he also felt
forgiving. The truth was, against the Utt, men had not
been that great, either.

As he had the thoughts, several women climbed onto
the distant stage. One of these walked forward, and said
something. Her words came to Grayson as a faraway
mumble. But the entire female audience greeted the
statement with a great cheer—as if they had heard
what she said.

The meeting continued in that same inaudible fashion. Apparently—so reasoned a disappointed Grayson
—the rest of the audience heard what was said by way
of a special ear device. And he and Miss Lesser (who

had come illegally) didn't. For this he was not prepared.

From the way the woman on the stage kept bowing, and putting her hands together in the prayer position, there seemed no question. It was indeed a religious service.

The Utt must have studied mankind's religions. And here in the "West" they had the Christian punishment-and-reward system. These women had become sexless angels. Than which no one could be more frigid . . . at least, that was his picture of the female body once it arrived in heaven—

Actually, it was a startling thing the invaders had done. They had taken a beautiful symbolic idea—heaven—and given it a location in space. And required of the worshippers a literal adherence to a Victorian interpretation of biblical saintly behavior.

Right now that had one excellent feature. He could do certain things. He could seek out the source of the spy ray. And this scientifically untrained mass of feminity wouldn't be able to stop him.

Grayson hadn't thought of himself as in the process of making up his mind. But, abruptly, there it was: decision.

He leaned toward Miss Lesser; whispered into her ear; "You stay here, and report to me later what happened. Particularly, notice how they get back to—" He stopped; figuratively teetered there verbally. He had been about to say, ". . . back to earth." Instead, he finished rather lamely, ". . . back to the parking area."

Having, in fact, said the right words, he recovered his decisiveness. And stood up energetically. Miss Lesser made the mistake, then, of turning her head and watching him as he maneuvered to get to the ceiling. It was a mistake because Grayson pulled his left overshoe sole free of its magnetic contact with the floor. Bent over. Put both hands on the floor. Jerked his other foot free, as if he were going to stand on his hands. And shoved with both arms.

Scientific know-how could do that for a person who

understood the reality involved. But as his body, thus propelled, rose effortlessly into the air, head "down," the young police woman's eyes widened. And then glazed.

Since she was still safely seated, Grayson turned his eyes away from her and from whatever turmoil she was experiencing.

And, temporarily, forgot her.

Chapter Twenty-six

For Grayson, who understood that this was an outer-space phenomenon, a world of no ups and no downs, there wasn't any sense of oddness. On arriving at the "ceiling," he placed his feet flat on *that* floor. So that if there was metal there, his overshoes would magnetically attach.

It was a great moment, then, when first his left foot, and then his right, actually made a clicking sound. And the ceiling-floor grabbed and held each in turn.

And so, there he stood, upside down in relation to everyone else. If any of the women looked up, they now saw a strange sight. A woman, head "down," walking in the clumping fashion of magnetic shoes across the ceiling. Where he-she was walking to was what, from a distance, appeared to be the head of a staircase.

It *was* the head of a staircase. Except, of course, it went down in relation to him, but to any watching women it was as if he now walked up into the ceiling. Where that took him was another floor. And now that there were no visible females, it was easier to accept that he was standing in a normal way on a normal floor.

What he had come down to was another of those floor areas that looked like a hotel lobby. His quick, darting gaze noticed at once that there were half a dozen corridors branching off from the "lobby." And that was not a problem. His direction finder remained fixed. Unerringly, he headed along the third corridor (from the right), past several doors. And then there, according to his "fix," was the door.

The door panel was gray and glossy, smooth and plastic-looking. As Grayson tentatively shoved at it, it opened with an unexpected mechanical action. Retreated five inches. Then lifted up out of sight. The portion of room that was thus revealed looked ordinary enough.

Normally, under the severe circumstances by which he had come here, Grayson would have paused to survey even the most harmless-appearing object or location. But the action of the door brought the thought that it might come gliding down as rapidly as it had gone up.

And so, with only a flick of his eyes this way and another flick that . . . he stepped across the threshold.

Even now, at his second look, the room seemed disappointingly ordinary. It had a few earth-type chairs. A table. A cot with a pillow at one end. A viewplate on one wall, and off to one side, an alcove leading to what he presumed was a clothes closet.

The appearance was, in fact, so mundane that Grayson had consciously to resist a feeling of relief. And, of course, his knowledge helped. This was an era of science where, even on earth—in fact, for his entire adult lifetime—electronic equipment had been miniaturized to the point of virtual invisibility.

Something from this room had noticed, was noticing, him. Whatever it was, the energy beam from the laser device in his shoulder padding put it out of commission. Yet it had at once repaired itself.

It was for the debris of that initial discharge that

he searched. To find it, he utilized a micro-computer with micro-attachments, all of which were glued under the middle finger of his left hand.

Which signaled him over to the viewplate on the wall. Grayson had to admit that was a location where one might expect to find a spy device. He knelt for a closer look.

A closer look? In a way, an impossibility—it turned out. This viewplate was designed to operate at several levels. That was what his expert eye saw, now that he was bending close. At the gross level, the instrument actually worked as a large screen for the well-known television channels. Below that, there was not just one, there were several additional divisions into progressively smaller systems.

The screen itself, Grayson noted, was made up of micro-instruments, hundreds of them. At least a thousand divisions-in-size below *that* was a mini-micro electro-world. On earth, mini-micro units were available for innumerable purposes; so that level was within his training.

But there was a fourth level of ultra-miniaturization embedded in the mini-micro instrumentation. That was not visible, as such, even with the special magnifying computer that he carried with him like an extra fountain pen. Its presence was implicit in the design of Level Three. And what that told a saddened Grayson —told him once again—was that here was a technology far beyond anything he knew.

Fortunately, the spy ray was at the second level. But there disappointment awaited him again. His aim had been all too accurate. There was a tiny burned area on the viewplate, close to the floor. And an energized dot on the floor itself. That turned out to be the hole the laser beam had drilled on its way to the real target.

Grayson straightened with the reluctant realization that all there was left to do was search this room, and the adjoining ones; and then return to Doris Lesser. Standing there, frustrated, his eyes took in the room several times. It was on the fifth of these rapid surveys that his attention finally focused on the clothes closet.

He went over, of course. And the alcove did not lead to a clothes closet at all. With suddenly widening eyes he found himself gazing at what, at close quarters, looked like the same bluish panel size and shape as the one on the thirty-fifth floor of the Heaven building on earth. There he had watched the Artificial Blonde reach forth with her arm and hand, and there he had reached in the same way.

At the time he had been too completely caught by surprise even to think of investigating the magical instrument. Now, he ought at least to find out what might be involved in a proper research job.

He put his hand out. Slowly. Inching it—millimetering it—forward. Suddenly, the tip of the long middle finger met resistance.

Grayson drew back, impressed. Right there, inches in front of the blue panel, something that registered as, of all things, a barrier.

Again, the extended hand and fingers. This time, at the exact location where he felt the . . . barrier . . . he pushed fractionally forward. Instantly something tried to grab the tip of the finger.

Grayson jerked back, startled.

All right, all right, so it's that violent.

It was already obvious that for the research task he would need instrumentation. So it was definitely something for later. After he had considered what instruments might be useful. Do it soon, naturally.

Too bad, in a way, but intellectually true that nothing should be done immediately. With that, he turned to leave the alcove. And, as he did so, heard a sound.

He was quick, then. He spun around on one heel. Thus, he had a fleeting glimpse of—of—

He came to in a small room, half-sitting, half-lying on a soft, rubbery floor. And his very first thought was: *What* was it? What did I see?

Nothing live. Whatever it was had glittered like a mirror mounted on— Wait! Not just one mirror. Thousands of little mirrors. Tiny, gleaming surfaces with pictures on them.

What stunned him was that he was suddenly realizing where the mirror-bright gleamings had originated. From the viewplate. The alcove and the viewplate were aligned. They were across the room from each other. And, somehow, he, who was usually so aware, hadn't noticed.

It was the fourth level of smallness—he analyzed. The matter transmitter in the alcove *needed* the assistance of that ultra-miniaturized system.

Needed it for what?—Sudden shock feeling.

He had the awful sinking sensation that such an alignment was utilized for extremely sensitive purposes. For refinements that were apparently not necessary in the transmission system used to get people to the orbiting station.

Where to? he thought, shaken. *Where to?*

It had felt different this time. Not like being grabbed, and shoved. Simply—blank—and here I am.

Slowly, Physicist Grayson, whose visible behavior was proof of the correctness of Utt theories about the human male, climbed to his feet. He was careful because he didn't quite know how his body would react. After a long moment—relief. No dizziness. Strength seemed normal. So he had survived the journey.

Standing up, he saw that this room was completely bare, except directly across from him was an entire wall of alcoves with recessed bluish panels. Uncertainly, not knowing what else to do, he counted them: one, two . . . fourteen.

It was an impressive total. Presumably, they could all take him somewhere. That brought an uneasy feeling, and a return of the thought, stronger this time: "Where am I, *now?*"

The first transport had taken him from the thirty-fifth floor of an earth building to an orbiting satellite thousands of miles away. This second one?—

Uneasily, he walked across the room, and paused a short distance from the array of other matter transmitters. Fourteen different places that he could go. That was instantly shaking. Because *so many* in one little room. Something of the vastness of what was here was in that awareness.

What do they do? he wondered. Bring these . . . transmitters . . . to a place like the solar system? And then they don't need to come by ship anymore?

There was a genuine door to his left. And he walked firmly toward it. No more journeys for Peter Grayson, thank you, until he knew exactly where he was, and exactly where he was heading next.

The door opened onto a corridor. The corridor led to the foot of a staircase.

It was strangely soothing going up a set of stairs at a time of bewilderment and anxiety. Grayson took two steps at a time, and saw that there was a turn up and ahead. It was a ninety-degree turn. As he started up that, he saw another turn ahead. And when he came to that, there was a door half a dozen steps away.

Doors were normally passageways to other locations. Maybe, if he opened this one, there would instantly be a clue to his present location. Besides, what else was there to do?

He emerged onto a flat stretch of white plastic material. It spread before him, vaguely yellowish in color, for a mile at least. Beyond that was a flat horizon, a sky that was tinted red.

It was, at once, an unearthly scene. And it brought the most terrible thought he had ever had in his whole life: This is not earth. This is not the solar system.

Chapter Twenty-seven

Grayson lay down.

Literally, he sagged onto that flat, gleaming surface. Turned over on his left side. And drew his knees up.

The feeling that came was that he was going to die.

A timeless period went by. During that inner darkness, even his body had no purpose. He was not even like a person who goes to sleep at night. Because the sleeping body conveys with its turns and twists that when the sleeper awakens, he will arrive at awareness with all his goals intact. Nothing like that here.

Afterward, he could deduce that only a few minutes were taken by the period of almost death. He could deduce that because, since he did not die (and was not unconscious), presently there were shadowy images flickering through his perception centers.

That first group of images consisted of a peculiar awareness. It was an in-his-mind visualization of a lean human body in woman's clothing lying on a flat surface. She was all scrunched. As if she had drawn up her knees. As if she were trying to squeeze her body into a ball-like shape. And almost succeeding.

It took a while for Grayson's dead-slow brain to realize that the fantasy had a reality in it: Good God, that's me!

More time went by. For a while he was astonished that his mind, all by itself, had worked out such a simulated visual image. But there was no question. . . . That is exactly what I must look like, lying here—

Another, less pleasant, awareness came: The proprioceptive system began to send him signals. The message was that he was lying on something hard. And—with progressive insistence—that he was also in an uncomfortable position.

Finally, like a sleeping person who comes vaguely awake for similar reasons of discomfort, the automaton who had once been Dr. Peter Grayson, physicist, groaned. And turned over.

That was the beginning. How long does it take to come out of shock so that there can be a thought about that shock? Again—afterward—he deduced that additional minutes went by. Only minutes, not hours. And then—

When it came, the thought was: I've just had the most basic terror a human being can experience. . . . He was a person no longer on his own planet. And he had no idea how to get back. Without help.

He couldn't dare take the chance of hoping that one of the fourteen alcoves, each with its matter transmitter, would return him to earth. So he would have to seek out—who? The Utt. Grayson quailed. Because in Utt eyes he was a sinner.

Nevertheless, the beginning of purpose was in that cringing thought. And what that purpose, carried out, might have led to, all by itself, was never put to the test.

For at that exact instant of time—a sound!

Something, or someone, shuffling.

The noise reached through all the murky distances in Grayson's mind. It penetrated past a hundred foggy images. The actual effect was as if a needle had been jabbed into him. He sat up. Suddenly.

And opened his eyes. "Uh!" he said.

Coming toward him across the plain of plastic was a two-legged, unhuman being. Not an Utt. This alien was about five and a half feet tall, and two feet wide in his mid-section. He had two arms, and he wore a shining covering over that pudgy body. There were gleaming metal attachments running all the way up his arms to the stocky shoulders. His face was a small blob below some kind of headgear from which two thin metal rods extended upward.

Grayson didn't have time to notice additional details. The sight of such a live specimen approaching him was sufficient motivation. He stood up. And, as the creature paused less than five feet away, it was Grayson who said, "Who are you?"

The words had a defensive purpose behind them. They were intended to be a small barrier. And, because one little question seemed instantly inadequate, he added, almost without pausing, "Where am I?"

The plump being reached over with his left hand to his right wrist. Only it was now, suddenly, not an arm but a tentacle—obviously nothing had changed except Grayson's awareness. Very carefully, next, with several thin tendrils which extended from the end of the tentacle, the creature adjusted a device that he wore like a wristwatch.

It was such a human action. So similar to what an earthman might have done, taking into account the state of technological art, that—just like that—a feeling of normalcy swept over Grayson.

He asked his third question in a tone of voice that was no longer a vocal extension of basic fear. He said, "Is this the home planet of the Utt?"

"Everybody away," was the reply.

The words came out in English from the tiny instrument which the alien had adjusted a few seconds earlier.

Grayson took the reply without having an unusual reaction. So far, no mysteries. Presumably, a computer had listened to his questions, consulted a memory bank, in which—awesome possibility—the languages of the galaxy were stored. And had responded at once.

The physicist was now convinced that this was Utt country. The entire sequence of his coming was meaningless if that were not true.

So he said, "Where are the Utt?"

"The masters?" Surprise. "Oh, they away doing good."

There was pride in the tone in which the words came out of the tiny wrist speaker. As Grayson reflected briefly on the meaning of the term "masters," the plump being went on: "Usually, somebody here. But today guidance needed all over. So all the bosses gone to do the good deed."

. . . Well, thought Grayson, with a return of that old wry emotion of his, I suppose it could be like that—

He needed the private thought to help him overcome a feeling that it really wasn't this simple. Everybody gone. *Everybody!* Every Utt away from his own planet, minding somebody else's business.

True—he grew calmer—the universe was a big place. It might even be that the hundred thousand million suns of the Milky Way galaxy had four billion inhabited planets. Enough to require the guidance of the equivalent in Utt of the entire human race.

But—Grayson took another look around the glistening artificial surface on which he and his informant stood. It was like a flat lake. And that was the puzzle. It was a relatively small lake. His impression: small number of Utt.

He said, "What are you called?"

"We are the servants of the masters." The same prideful tone. "We qualified, no one else."

Grayson decided not to be detoured from his immediate purpose by those implications. "How many of you are there?" he asked. And that was pretty sly; since, if he got that answered, he could deduce the Utt population.

"Oh, it take 1,200,000 of us for each Utt."

Grayson's mind did one of those darting actions. A brain-searching mechanism darted into hundreds of byways of his memory storing systems. The search was for a clue to the meaning that had just been projected at and into his hearing centers.

He drew a complete blank.

Finally, sadly, he thought: All right, all right, so much for the sly approach.

Presently, he wondered: If I were going to guide the Utt in the way they guided human beings, what would I now deduce to be the problem to be solved?

On earth, the Utt had decided that the male human had caused *all* of the problems. Which, Grayson had already agreed within himself, had a certain truth.

On Utt-World, the only visible Achilles' heel was standing in front of him: the proud slave.

Ready to do or die, Grayson thought.

He intended sarcasm. Instead, his attention focused on the final word of his thought. What was stunning, he had used an English stereotype (do or die). And the reality of the "die" part reached up, and out, and hit him with its grim meaning. On earth, tyrants had always been able to find a foul crew to over-serve them. And do-gooders, given power, had historically proved to be the equals of the worst tyrants.

He took a step backward.

It was his first move toward escape. Somehow, the Utt servant and he had got awfully close to each other. As he recalled it, the chunky had edged nearer to him, one shuffle at a time.

Figuratively, then, his mind flipped through its files. He was seeking words that would delay a servant from acting. "I'm from earth," he said.

It was Ploy Number One. The use of the truth to prepare the way for the coming connivance. "On earth," he added, "we call ourselves human beings."

"I know," said the creature. "I focus camera at you, and computer whisper in my . . ."—it pointed at the antenna gear on its head—". . . what kind you be."

Grayson decided to assume that he was winning. Both

his statements, and the reply, were within the frame of his plan. So he took another step backward, and said, "I don't know the name of the Utt who, uh, guides"— [always use the language of the other side]—"us human beings, but—"

He paused, hopeful. The hope had to do with the possibility that maybe there was only one Utt. If so, please, Mr. Servant, don't notice that I'm fishing for information, and please give the information without noticing.

The wait grew too long. So he braced himself, and prepared for battle. And continued: "Under the circumstances of everybody being away, will you tell the guide for earth that Dr. Peter Grayson was here?—"

The wide being made a movement with its upper torso, and said, "Yes, I tell Master of Earth what you say."

Grayson had thought he had made his peace with the way the computer translated into English. But those accepting words had, not just one, but several connotations.

One of the implications was that the servant had, *this very minute,* told the Utt guide for earth about Dr. Grayson. Had, in fact, just barely finished telling the Utt.

The other connotation actually had to do with the language. Consciously, Grayson mentally savored three different interpretations: Master *of* Earth. Master *for* Earth. The particular master of this servant, who was the guide for earth.

The last one, he decided, soothed him somewhat.

As he experienced that feeling of mild relief, the computer voice sounded again, ending the brief silence there on that otherwise deserted plastic plain. It said, "I have just now receive instructions from the Master about you."

That was a meaning that he could not allow to go by. "What you're saying"—pause for careful wording— "just now, from light-years away, by some kind of instant transmission, you received a message from the Utt who is now on earth?"

The servant did not seem to be aware of the shock that his prisoner was experiencing. For the computer's next words were: "Master say problem of what to do with you very severe. First human being who has ever found this planet. Decision will have to be made, pretty basic. But it will be done private. Between you and he. Personal meeting."

Grayson was amazed to realize that he was relieved.

He stood there on that plastic roof—what else could it be but a roof?—and savored the words that, for a few moments, had sounded like *the end had come*. Almost at once, the meaning had changed inside him to: he would continue to be alive until he was taken back through a matter transmitter by way of the earth satellite connection. From there, he would go to the thirty five-story, high-rise building at the far south end of the city. Then add automobile transportation time to his office.

A two-hour journey, he decided, give or take twenty minutes.

Even more important, there was no danger, anymore, here. Orders had arrived from the boss. So Do or Die no longer had an immediate threat in it—if, indeed, it had ever existed at all anywhere but in his overheated imagination.

. . . Maybe, with two huge hours to pass, I can either test out my equipment against this servant, or—better still—talk the poor, deluded nut out of the whole notion of one intelligent life form being a servant to another—

Start a slave revolution!

As these almost flippant, and definitely over-stimulated thoughts and feelings flitted through his consciousness, Grayson took another, longer look at his guard.

There was the same bulky body, positively repulsive. Somehow, the creature suddenly reminded him of a bejeweled fat man on earth, whose jewels only emphasized the ugly fat. The Utt servant's arm-tentacles glittered from shoulder to wrist with a plethora of metallic devices. Worse, a sheath of gleaming fabric covered the ungainly body. It was a thick material, and it added additional appearance of size to the already ridculously large middle. And, topping all this glop, was a pudgy face, half-hidden—thank God—under overhanging electronic headgear. The face had two black eyes, high up, very close together. Awful. Incredible. But—

It was either time to decide that such a being deserved to be a slave, or time to start inciting.

"I suppose," Grayson said, "you're one of the technically trained *slaves* of the Utt."

"All we Orsolites," was the reply, "are technical."

The great word came out of the computer. The pronunciation was clear and unmistakable. The marvelous implication: . . . That's the name of this servant race. And he finally came out with it, and didn't notice—

It was a tiny victory, in a way. But it had taken all these minutes to get; and Grayson was briefly held breathless. A name from a distant part of the galaxy. Definitely, it was not nothing.

"Now"—into that brief silence came the voice; and a tentacle pointed off to one side—"please, you walk over maybe five long steps. Out of way."

Momentary sense of defeat. Control was thus swiftly taken away from him. It was instantly, of course, a mystery. A small mystery, perhaps, but not obviously threatening.

Silently, thinking hard, Grayson obeyed the instruction. When he came to the fifth step, he turned. And waited.

"My thanks," said the voice. "Distance transmission need more precaution. More care."

It was suddenly a sinking-inside moment. The gaunt human male in woman's clothes stood there, startled. The explanation had an immediacy sound to them.

What was all this nonsense about walking five steps out of the way? There was no visible sign of anything to be out of the way of.

To every horizon, as far as Grayson could see, was

flat country. True, the place had its own appeal. A mile-long, mile-wide, plastic covering—Grayson deduced—for an underground city.

Strange, beautiful, desolate planet of the race that was guiding all intelligent life in the galaxy because they knew how things should be. Up there, the marvelous reddish sky. And, down here, beyond the yellowish plastic, no hills, no visible water, nothing alive on all this emptiness except this one Utt servant and this single human being.

Somebody ought to explore the planet. It was always valuable to know something about a dominant race. Maybe—sudden, anxious, recollection of purpose—if I could get the revolution started . . .

No time, anymore, for the indirect approach. Grayson said, hoarsely, "On earth, sir, we human beings long ago made slavery illegal. In some instances, wars had to be fought to enforce freedom—"

His voice, there on that deserted plain, faltered.

Out of nowhere, something. Slightly off to one side, it was. So he saw it first out of the corner of one eye. He blinked, and turned, and saw . . . a bluish panel, higher than his head. It stood there, straight up, right out in the open where, instants before, there had been nothing. It seemed to be embedded in the roof. Could it have slid into view from a hidden slot while he was engrossed in the scenic blah that surrounded them on every side?

Obvious, now, that this was why he had been asked to step "out of the way." And what was teeth-grinding was that he had done it again. Once again, at a key moment, his attention drawn off.

Before he could think, or chide himself, further, the computer-translator said, "We Orsolites develop technical systems for quick travel because, when have hundred thousand planets for keeping in touch, ordinary transport too slow. Instant method needed. So, now, short trip, simple. But long trip still need extra sensitive—"

The speaker broke off, sharply: "Watch, please! No step back farther!"

Grayson had been retreating automatically, an inch-by-inch backward shuffle. As the voice went up in volume so abruptly, he halted, startled. And looked behind.

"Good Lord!" he spoke aloud.

It was a viewplate. Like the one that had been aligned with the blue panel on the orbiting satellite.

And he was standing between the two. Between the panel in front and the viewplate behind. *That* was where he had walked, not out of the way but in the way.

As he teetered there, confused, the chunky creature spoke once again through the computer on its arm: "Utt Master have similar system in your office on earth. So, if you now walk up to panel—"

"Just a minute," said Grayson, vaguely.

He saw that the chunky Orsolite was staring at him with his jet-black eyes. And the creature seemed to be prepared to wait, though perhaps not a whole minute.

"You mean to tell me—" Grayson began. Once more, his words dwindled before the vast inner silence he was experiencing. He stood there. And the simulations set in motion past his mind's eye, visualized a galactic civilization, comprising tens of thousands of inhabited planets. And one people—the Orsolites—attaining technological mastery of space and time. And then—

The minute was evidently up. For the voice of the chunky super-being came through the computer again, saying now: "We take over whole Milky Way galaxy. And then on one planet—this one—we find the Utt saints. They have nothing physical. We have everything. They live, each to his hut. We live in magnificent cities. When we talk, we suddenly realize they have answer we don't have. All our big machine civilization have no purpose. So—everybody agree—we put our system behind their good. They go out with our help, and guide everybody, everywhere, to the way life should be for each. The pure way."

At that point, finally, Grayson said, "Uh!"

And he added, sadly, "And it takes about 1,200,000 of you to back up one Utt."

"It work out that way. We keep interstellar civilization going, and do what necessary. Very satisfy in the heart."

Grayson had one final desperate thought: that blue sun, juxtapositioned with earth in the "hell" part of, I presume, each big city—what's it there for?

Pause. Then: "Some time even Utt give up on a life group, and send the order to exterminate unacceptable species and their planet. Unhappily, we carry out instruction, and blow up the whole system. For the good of the galaxy."

The tentacle pointed again. "That way, Dr. Grayson. Walk up close to the—"

The word for the name of the matter transmitter in the Orsolite language—the earthman deduced from the sound and the context—was "bratata."

Grayson did not resist. His plan, at the moment of crisis, to pit the concealed equipment he had in and on his body against the equipment of the Utt servant, had suffered a fateful diminishment. He had no illusions. His hope had been that earth physics would have a chance against the scientific knowledge allowed to a slave. Instead, these Orsolites in a stunning revelation were suddenly identified as the super-scientists.

It was too much too quickly. And that brought just a touch of his occasional mild mad humor. So that, as he walked toward the blue panel, slightly hampered by his female dress, mincing a little, at the moment when the blankness hit him, he was thinking: The next monster you will see is—

Chapter Twenty-eight

How scared should you be of an alien who has been around nearly four decades, and during that time has not killed any human except some of its own rebellious servants?

The only problem was that this alien had been quoted by a reliable authority—one of his (its) Orsolite "servants" on Utt-World—that, for one man, for Peter Grayson, there would have to be a basic decision.

The Utt Master for Earth looked like a large, bearded frog, complete with spindly legs and arms. And like a frog, he (it) had two eyes, high up and near the sides of the head.

. The creature sat behind a desk, which had a unique quality of appearing to be completely transparent. Since the room was brightly lighted, the Utt was visible through it, almost as if there was nothing there. What made the virtual invisibility of the desk even more special was, if the desk had drawers with anything in them . . . it didn't show. Either the light was cunningly guided around the drawers. Or else nothing like that was allowed to clutter or offend the visual perfection.

Off to the left in one corner was the now familiar blue panel of a matter transmitter. It was that panel through which, only minutes earlier, Grayson had come from Utt-World. The panel was aligned with the equally familiar, four-level viewplate, needed as an aide in interstellar transmission.

This latter instrument, inch-thick, and long and fairly narrow, seemed to be firmly attached to the wall in the opposite corner.

What, in those first minutes, after he had been directed to sit at his own desk, continued to disturb the physicist was the realization that the desk and the transmitter combination must have been deliberately moved into his office. As arranged, presumably purposefully, the Utt's desk faced his own. The Utt accordingly sat with his back to the door of the outer office.

When? Why? What?—

The presence of the desk, and the way the thin viewplate had already been affixed to a wall, somehow emphasized the word the Orsolite had used . . . earlier: Basic.

Something permanent was about to happen. Beginning with the, uh, basic act of taking over this inner scientific sanctum of the Haskett laboratory complex.

The chief scientist of that company inwardly braced himself. His tense thought: I'll fight before I let anything genuinely negative be done. But he didn't really know what he meant by that.

On top of the transparent, beautiful desk facing Grayson was a small metal object. From it, a voice said, "It has been interesting to us to observe what changes have been made in our original rules."

The computer that made the statement in good English spoke in a flat, emotionless tone. If the Utt had, in fact, found anything "interesting," the enthusiasm was not transmitted by the machine.

And the meaning itself was relatively unthreatening. Grayson actually had time to deduce that this particular translation computer had probably been made for earth languages in relation to the Utt tongue. Whereas, the one used by the Orsolite way off there in interstellar space must be adjusted for millions of languages in a simple fashion.

Also, he wondered how a single Utt could have observed the changes so secretly undertaken by a small group of individuals in one small corner of the planet. Grayson let that mystery go by, for the moment. And, still, no decision.

The voice continued: "But the fact that the changes were primarily made by male human beings makes them suspect."

That instantly had the sound of crisis coming fast.

The speaker belonged to a race of beings who, during forty years, had proved that, as a "guide," he acted on what he believed.

Within that frame, "suspect" became a word of total power.

Yet it still didn't sound too "basic." Besides, he was a man who had recently confronted many crises; and also he had his techniques. He said, now, in his best positive approach, "Do any of the changes meet with your approval? And, if so, which?"

And that, likewise, had no plan in it, except for the vague possibility that it might create a delay.

The voice was silent. The frog eyes had wandered, and seemed thoughtful. They were gazing pensively past the man. Or so it seemed. It was a little difficult to determine where a frog was looking; but the eyes *had* shifted.

Then: "We accept," said the voice box, "the change in the criminal law as to who shall be incarcerated. And accept that those who administer the jails shall be entitled to visit the surface. The concept of equality between prisoner and jailer in the old rules seems to violate an instinct for ascendancy in the human make-up."

It took a reach of the mind just to grasp that thought. . . . Is he—it—saying that the person who has the job of restraining a criminal should be required to live under similar restraint?

"However," the voice continued, "we must insist

that the visits be limited to an eight-hour period once a week."

An unhappy mental picture marched past Grayson's mind's eye: himself at the next meeting of the leaders telling the Zolohoffs and the others that they would have to move back into the pit.

But it had the sound of a firm decision. And, no question, it was the end of the first stage of this fantastic confrontation between a human being and an Utt.

And it was a step backward.

Stage Two started well.

A thought. Grayson noticed the single, most significant, positive quality about the new ruling: it did not affect him, personally.

What he did not notice was the significance of that awareness.

The to-me-ness of human life was not something to which he had ever really paid attention. And it had definitely not occurred to him in his whole adult life that government was fundamentally a continuous, day-and-night struggle to hold back, to level off, to compensate for the ceaseless pressure from nearly four billion egos, each of which was as self-absorbed as he.

Now—his instantly hopeful feeling: If this is the level of critical comment from the Utt Master for Earth, then I can stop trembling.

And no drastic decision on his part was even remotely called for.

Belatedly, since he wanted to look good at some future time, it occurred to him that his system of dialogue required that he make defensive points on behalf of the people who would be affected by the ruling.

But that was actually a technique, and not yet a decision.

He heard his voice, then, speak the defense: "May we discuss that point later, sir? But, first, are there any other rule changes that you find acceptable?"

Silence. After he had spoken.

There they sat, each at his desk, facing each other. The Utt, with 1,200,000 Orsolite servants to back him up. And Peter Grayson, human being, essentially with nothing but his little methods.

Once more, the appearance was of the alien staring past him as if in some deep, private thought.

Considering new guidelines for earth, no doubt.

It was a faintly sarcastic reaction. But there was no purpose in it. Grayson was still like a prisoner in the dock. Only he was his own defense attorney; and so he knew that his defense was actually limited to a few sales techniques.

Before the grim reality of that could penetrate, the voice box spoke again: "The human male seems to have discovered a decisive loophole in the system we devised to protect the people of earth from his primitive needs. Naturally, in his ancient, evil fashion, those persons involved in the loophole have taken full advantage."

"Huh!" said Grayson. And then he shuddered. For he had just heard genuine attack statements. He parted his lips—for what was not clear. Somehow, he restrained the words that wanted to pour out. Restrained them because it would be absolutely awful if he assumed he knew what the Utt was talking about. And by replying thereby gave the creature information it didn't have.

The Utt's machine voice went on: "Since the method of resistance has been spread all over the planet, the solution will have to be more radical than anything that has hitherto been undertaken."

Even as that threat was transmitted by the voice box, the individual who made it sat in his chair behind his almost invisible desk. And, incredibly, he (it) radiated goodwill, compassion, kindness, and an all-encompassing benign attitude of blessing everybody.

A fleeting thought touched Grayson's cringing mind: Was this the way the members of the Inquisition had felt about themselves in those minutes before, in the name of God, they sentenced the condemned to be burned at the stake?

It must have been something like that. Because here,

also, was a creature who apparently accepted on the silent level of internal no-thinking that he (it) knew what was best for everybody. And acted accordingly.

Far, far better if the Orsolites had bestowed their science and technology upon other intelligent races including mankind. Surely, that was the real road to ultimate understanding of the meaning of all things. Above all, spare us from do-gooders.

Within that frame of reason, he made another defensive statement. He said, "I presume, sir, you refer to the act of copulation by a human man and woman. Since you exist, I deduce that the Utt race also reproduces. I would consider it privileged information if you would reveal the method."

Silence.

Once again it was hard to determine if his request had temporarily diverted the alien being from its own purpose. Abruptly, confirmation. And the fantastic answer.

"An Utt female," said the voice, "is in heat every fifty earth years. In all of this galaxy, we have never observed a purer method of propagation in an intelligent species. And what obviously proves its perfection is that it is the only natural method which also provides virtual immortality for those who were privileged to be born Utt."

It occurred to a resigned Grayson that his dialogue system had never before been required to react to an ego that offered total proof of perfection.

Because he knew such details, at that point he experienced a swift fantasy. Did the male Utt sit on top of the female Utt in the manner of an earth frog? When a frog laid its egg, it was the job of the male to fertilize it from its on-top position as it emerged.

That was about as saintly as the act of reproduction could be—it seemed to Grayson.

The thought faded. The creature was stirring again. More decisions? If so, none were his own. Yet.

"Let us get to the main point," said the voice box. "I refer to your own recent aggressive behavior. Unfortunately for you, you have discovered a route to our planet. There are two possible solutions. One, a change in the transmission channel group. I understand from our servant race, the Orsolites, that that would require innumerable modifications of the entire system in this area of space. The alternative is that we provide one human being—yourself—with another place of residence. As you may deduce, that is by far the best method. Accordingly, it is my judgment that you be removed from earth forever. You will be sent to some planet of equal technologic development, there to live out what remains of your admittedly short life."

It was that brief. That direct.

The blankness that descended on Grayson as the verdict hit him precipitated an involuntary response. He was like a person, as he sat there, stunned, who has recently moved from a long-time residence to a new home. And during moments when his attention is elsewhere he unthinkingly heads for the old place.

All these moments he had been bracing himself to act, if necessary—intending it to be a conscious decision.

It wasn't. In his mental state, he now automatically activated the first stage of his attack: a mechanism that discharged a frozen-gas needle at his enemy.

The tiny glinting object struck the upper right arm. And it appeared to do exactly what it was supposed to: entered the flesh, and instantly dissolved.

Having fired the weapon, Grayson realized what he had done. Suddenly. Like the man who actually arrives at his old home before the truth dawns on him that he doesn't live here anymore.

In this instance, there was the immediate shocking realization that he had made an attack to which he was now committed.

In that awful moment of shocked awareness, he saw that the Utt seemed to be disturbed. The creature's great eyes ceased to stare past where Grayson sat.

. . . No escape.

Grim now, Grayson fired a second weapon. This one

was an invisible light ray of a very high frequency designed to interfere with certain functions of the brain.

Three more discharges followed, all of them—like the first two—essentially quick, silent, unobtrusive. So much so that human beings never noticed. His hope: that the Utt likewise would be only vaguely aware.

As he waited for reaction, the Utt voice continued: "Human beings have apparently found many ways of evading our simple, pure guidance system. It is, therefore, my judgment that in this one situation only—earth—I shall instruct our trained servants, the Orsolites, to take action. They will forthwith occupy this planet, and for a period provide closer supervision of all male activities until the nature of male human recalcitrance has been determined, and a permanent rectification made—"

All through *that* speech Grayson sat in total dismay. His entire attack system had had no visible effect. Among other things, the system was designed to produce forgetfulness—and there was, instead, total continuing memory. It was designed to create fantasies; and in human beings it did so create; but there was no sign of such in the Utt. It was designed to render unconscious, as it had rendered The Revolution. But there the creature sat. Unaffected. Alert in his fashion. Meaning, still pensive. Still not looking at his victim.

And at that point it made the devastating explanation: "Our Orsolite servants made a study of the body implant weapons by which you entered, and escaped, from the underground prison for male criminals. Naturally, they forthwith proofed me against such. So these systems will not be useful to you in our confrontation here today."

Grayson parted his dry lips, and croaked, "May we discuss that? Now, is there any other change in our rules that you find—?"

He stopped, utterly astounded at himself. All his basic "cool" was gone, as those words had proved. There he had done it, mouthing modifications of the patter he used at business conventions, in company personnel meetings, with salesmen when they sat in the chair facing the mirror, and—

The feeling of total defeat struck through him, and was penetrating his remotest inner being, when—

A signal. In the recessed visiplate of his desk communicator.

The sensation from that instantly replaced the previous emotion. Like an electric shock.

In the past this was the way in which Miss Haskett had contacted him when he was in conference, and she wanted to speak to him.

As he sat there, petrified, a typed message showed silently on the lighted plate:

EVERYBODY IS HERE—THE ZOLOHOFFS, THE REVOLUTION IN FORCE—ALL HEAVILY ARMED. READY TO BREAK IN AT YOUR SIGNAL.

For tiny fractions of a second, hope came. And then, unfortunately, memory moved through Grayson's mind. It was the memory of the original arrival of the Utt.

The great ship, the colossal miles-long ship, had come. The huge thunder of its engines poured down upon the deafened populations of New York, and Washington, and Moscow, and London, and other cities— for it cruised everywhere—and after about a month, an Utt came down, and took over.

No one resisted.

The President and his cabinet handed over the White House.

The Praesidium of the Soviet Union walked out of the Kremlin.

Everywhere, governments abdicated.

Not a shot was fired.

An Utt spoke on an international TV hookup, and announced the Utt purpose was to make earth peaceful and prosperous, and to create a world of justice and truth. . . .

That was the memory. It had been a kaleidoscopic recollection, after the manner of such things; and, of course, now he knew that the ship must have been an Orsolite super-battleship; and that it was these "servants" who had silently behind the scenes utilized their science to overwhelm the minds of government leaders.

From the moment that he noticed Miss Haskett's message through the entire memory, required seconds only. And, of course, he realized that the people in the outer office, with their weaponry, whatever it might be, didn't have a chance.

Nevertheless, it was an indecisive Grayson that glanced up with glazed eyes. And found brief relief.

The Utt was staring past him at the rear wall, apparently in deep thought again.

Grayson reached over casually into the recessed space of the desk communicator, and printed on it: "WAIT!"

And at that very instant, a thought. Because—

He noticed *for the first time* what the Utt was doing, had been doing, all these minutes.

The mirror!

Incredible that not once until now had he remembered. Because, of course, that's why the so-and-so has got his desk facing this way.

The entranced monster was looking at his image in the great, mad mirror that spread its gleaming, silvery multi-self across the entire wall behind Grayson.

In its time, the mirror had probably reflected four thousand selves in the forms of faces and bodies, and eight thousand eyes. Brown eyes, blue, gray, hazel, and probably even green, all with one common obsession. Every pair had, over and over, glanced at the image of the person who owned the eyes, as that image reflected each shift of body, each attempt to sit more handsomely in the chair, to present a better appearance, casually to straighten a lock of hair, a twisted tie, or unwanted crease.

And, of course, never noticing the tens of thousands of tiny flickering hypnotic lights that Grayson had turned on with an equally casual reach of his hand under his desk.

Which flicking motion he made now.

And mentally poised there, awed by the colossal possibilities of the opportunity.

Suppose the Orsolite "servants" had not considered the mirror a weapon. And that this Utt had not been "proofed" against hypnotism.

At once, with that immense thought, Grayson's mind leaped back to a moment of key truth. Back there on the Utt planet, the sudden dazzling revelation. That wonderful moment when he realized that the Orsolites were the super-scientists; not the Utt.

. . . The utter vulnerability of a non-scientist type—

Like the first savage of long-ago earth, struck by a bullet, he would never realize what had hit him.

Sitting there, warm with his overwhelming awareness, Grayson abruptly realized it wasn't like that at all. In that initial moment of conflict between two cultures, the poor, dumb savage merely lost his tiny, precious life. But here, now:

. . . I could be deciding the future of the human race—

Let's not be too hasty, Grayson thought shakily.

The Utt had, beyond all question, proved one thing: When people believed there was a higher power, they behaved themselves.

It would be sheer insanity to take away that surrogate god completely. Besides, the Orsolites would be suspicious if he did an extreme reversal.

With that sobering realization, Grayson began his patter.

"There are many good things," he said, "in what the Utt have done for human beings. Many of the rules are excellent and should be continued. However, a solution ought to be found for the personal relationship situation of the excess female population in all parts of the world. Here, on the West Coast of the United States" —smoothly—"we have, as you know, set up a committee which has temporarily taken a compassionate personal attitude toward a few deprived—that is, unmarried—women. My suggestion is that the committee be assigned the power to select males on some merit basis which"—hastily—"we shall have to work out—in a private way as surrogate husbands. As you may know, in the past, before the Utt transformed earth into its present superior condition, such surrogate actions were undertaken entirely by chance. And so, many individual females were not included in the process at all. My suggestion is that future surrogate activity be guided by the committee in such a way as to include all deprived females."

Grayson's voice poised. He half—fearfully—expected a reaction. But there was nothing. Those big eyes continued to stare at the ugly—to Grayson—Utt shape in the mirror.

"It also would be advisable," Grayson went on, shakily, "if you trusted me, and reversed your judgment about my leaving earth. I should, of course, be given the right to travel by, uh, bratata, anywhere in the galaxy, and be provided with all needed special equipment. And, also, key committee members ought to have their lives prolonged by the best methods available. This"—smoothly—"would provide a continuity of administration, which has been lacking in the past, and"—glibly—"is probably responsible for many of the shortcomings which we have all noticed in human behavior. And I would further suggest that you visit earth at least once every twenty-five years. At which time additional decisions can be made, augmenting these recommendations. Finally, now that these basic decisions have been made, have your servant race disconnect earth from that blue sun at all stations where such connections were established. This precaution is no longer needed—"

His voice teetered there, so to say. Principally because he could think of nothing else to say, and also because more would not be advisable.

And he wondered desperately: Was the Utt just being polite? Was the creature listening, in the hope of gaining information. . . ? I really gave out plenty, by implication—

It didn't matter. If this failed, there was no other hope.

The man hesitated. And then, tense, he deliberately repeated the entire patter as well as he could remember it and in his best suggestive voice.

When *that* produced no reaction, his heart retreated just a little bit from the place high up in his throat where it felt as if it had lodged itself. Whereupon, he said it all again. And a third time.

After his fourth repetition, he flicked off the little pulsing lights. Reached over. And pushed a book that was lying on one side; pushed it off the desk.

The book hit the floor with a sound similar to the clapping together of a hypnotist's hands. And Grayson said, "Sir, it's up to you to make your final decision."

The frog-like being stirred. And said, "I have been reconsidering this earth situation, and I think I have arrived at a better solution.

"Perhaps," the creature continued, "we have been too rigid in our marriage requirements. The fact that females outnumber men does seem to create stress in those who have to remain single.

"I now believe," the Utt said, "that such and other details should be resolved by a committee of human beings, headed by yourself. Additional committees, under your jurisdiction, shall be set up in the distant parts of the planet; and the members of such committees as well as other selected persons—selected by you—shall be given methods of life prolongation, so that their experience is not lost by the early death situation common to the present human condition.

"You will be our contact, and may visit other star systems. An Orsolite will arrive at some convenient time, and explain the system of travel."

The Utt climbed awkwardly to its spindly feet. "I shall visit your office on this same date twenty-five years from now. We can discuss additional changes at that time."

The creature waddled over to the instrument that appeared to be—and, in fact, Grayson later discovered that it was—permanently attached to the floor in that corner.

"This will take me," it said, "to the orbiting space station. From there I can make my jump home."

Grayson, who had been breathing ever so slowly, almost as if he didn't dare make the slightest move— for fear of causing a distraction—said with the last bit of air in his lungs, "Good luck, sir."

Then he took a deep breath, and added hastily, "And thank you for sharing your wisdom and compassion with us. I—"

His words trailed off. Because the Utt was turning. . . . Oh, my God, did I lay it on too thick, even for him—?

The great eyes were staring—at him? It wasn't for sure. In his general direction? Definitely.

This time Grayson held his breath. And waited, desperate and afraid.

Over on the desk, the voice machine said, "The logical conclusion of our decisions here today will probably lead to earth being admitted to the galactic union much sooner than I had originally anticipated. Within a hundred years, probably."

"Uh," managed Grayson, "we shall, uh, await your advice."

His thought was: . . . Of course, I should have realized—One of the observations that had been made of hypnotized persons was that, afterward, they felt a need to act on the logic of what they had done. Either explain the act. Or carry on as if it had been a perfectly sensible thing to do.

The Utt was staring at him. "Under the circumstances," it said, "I shall instruct our servant race to disconnect this planet from certain precautionary destruct systems."

Bare moments after that, the Utt stepped forward. And was gone.

Gone for twenty-five years. For the moment, it felt like forever. Long enough to draw many a relieved breath.

It was still hard to believe a few moments later as he sank down in his chair, and called Miss Haskett. "You may all come in now," he said.

Already, his mind was rolling with thoughts of exactly how much, and what, he would tell the others.

Less than an hour later, he also stepped through the bratata to the orbiting space station. And not too many minutes after that he had located Miss Lesser, who was trying very hard to be brave. This, in spite of the fact that she had been alone in the vast, deserted room that the Utt had converted into heaven.

Seeing him, she was at once her brisk self again.

It appeared that Miss Lesser had yielded to her aggressive instincts. And she had told a tiny fib, and had asked a question.

The fib: This was her first time in heaven (that part, of course, was true, even though her presence was illegal), and she had got separated from her "guide" (in a manner of speaking, that was the fib).

The question, naturally, was: What was all this about?

The answer (from the three different women she asked): This was where young women were brought right after marriage to be indoctrinated to be "good" in the old Victorian sense.

. . . Boy! thought Grayson, lips compressing. From what he had heard, it was bad enough the way women normally became frigid after marrying the kind of dull clod that he had once been—

Miss Lesser, it turned out, had also watched how the other women left the place.

And so, presently, they were in her car driving down the ramp and into an earth city . . . that was still not exactly free— No human male had ever permitted that —Grayson acknowledged silently.

"But"—complacently—"considering what, as a man, I *could* have suggested, I was pretty sensible."

And, although his situation was now that of a male with a loving wife and three grateful mistresses, the right to do as he pleased, in a manner of speaking total con-

trol over earth, and with the power to bestow prolongation of life, and many now vague future possibilities of a vast nature; all of which he had grabbed for
himself with instant, instinctive, and total possessive-
ness . . . he really believed that.

Still—it was interesting to him occasionally that, in
the final issue, right down there at the nitty-gritty level
of decision-making, he had acted on some deep belief
that religion was a good thing.

For other people.

Great SF Authors

Great Science Fiction from Pocket Books

THEODORE STURGEON

A.E. VAN VOGT

JACK VANCE

KATE WILHELM

JACK WILLIAMSON

b SFG